CW00828938

Crime Comes

To The Cul De Sac

Beatrice Felicity
Cadwallader-Smythe

"If I am not who you say I am - then you are not who you think you are." - James Baldwin

"…in a capitalist society, racism functions as a means of divide and rule." - Yuris Prasad, Socialist Worker, July 23rd, 2022

"Whenever you run into it, prejudice always obscures the truth." - spoken by the character 'Davies' as played by Henry Fonda, in the film *12 Angry Men*.

"If I can just be myself I will be content." - Anne Frank, 1941.

With thanks to all those involved in the making of the films mentioned in this story which have enhanced the characters' lives and my own - with apologies that I cannot name them all.

CONTENTS

Chapter One
The Visit

It was all going swimmingly, apart from a few slight misunderstandings about territory and boundaries in a shared house: including one or two downright inexcusable oversights by Angela when her dual roles as hostess and landlady during the much anticipated, some would say dreaded, visit by her surprisingly domesticated son, his secret wife and their four, until quite recently, totally unknown-about children, somewhat clashed with her, no doubt, quite genuinely heartfelt roles as doting mother, quite surprised mother-in-law, and unsuspecting granny but it was nothing that a quick re-juggling of room and sleeping arrangements couldn't solve, helped by my own temporary decampment to a cosy B&B, which I had good reason to remember with some fondness from recent and more risqué days, plus a certainly unplanned, but very pleasurable reunion with my delighted, and still delightful, lover whom I had, after all, missed somewhat since deciding to once and for all end our illicit relationship now it had become, with the unexpected departure of my husband into his own lover's arms, totally licit.

Originally the plan was for me to decamp from the larger of the several bedrooms, into which I had moved a few months previously as Angela's new lodger, to allow the older children to share and for the younger ones to be ensconced in the room next to their parents' which was Angela's son, Hugo's, own room from his childhood and teenage years – complete with black, silver, and purple décor. This was the room into which I had willingly moved but although perfectly appealing and comfortable by day, it became a kind of insomniac's Hellhole at night and I had objected.

"But we could put blinds up," suggested Angela, when I explained about the street-lamp at the front of the house pouring its radiant orange glory wholeheartedly into the room (all night) unimpeded by the flimsy, silky curtains which I had initially thought so tasteful but which, like so many first impressions, had betrayed me in the night.

"But it's wildlife – they come over from off the common, and they are quite rare," Angela had helpfully pointed out when I had explained about the screech owl which, in the early hours, had been either serenading its spouse or celebrating its victories over the local mouse population – it was hard to decide which.

"But that's a pedigree show-dog, it's worth a fortune. The neighbours across the way breed them – they sell for thousands," was her equally farcical defence of the canine cacophony which regularly destroyed the brief, precious early morning owl- and streetlight-free nanosecond of blissful sleep. This was of course in between the streetlight switching off and the postie arriving on some diabolical errand or other at the house opposite – at which provocation the over-priced Hell-hound, which apparently made that house its lair, erupted in song loud enough to wake a thousand exhausted lodgers and destroy as many friendships.

I left for the B&B and gave Simon a ring. He was gratifyingly pleased to hear from me. There was still a 25-year age gap between us but, if it didn't bother him, I was determined to at least put up a good fight to prevent it ever bothering me.

The visit of the family from Canada, Angela's emigrant son and his until recently secret family of wife and children/step-children, had been an interesting three weeks for everyone. I had, of course, played the part of supportive friend, even co-baby-sitter, to perfection – plus occasionally joining in with outings as honorary aunt and providing the extra transport. I'd stepped in and taken them all to the park on the afternoons when Angela had had to attend her online seminars and watch the various films for her Film Appreciation 101 course. (Her love affair with the celluloid world had continued, showing no signs of being displaced with regard for this more inconvenient, less well-written, and real one – except when playing Hide and Seek with her newly acquired grandkids or strolling in the countryside on the other side of town with her son Hugo and his wife, Mafwaney.)

Despite all anticipation to the contrary of the three-week visit by her son and new (to her) daughter-in-law, Angela had avoided having the much-anticipated nervous breakdown in the kitchen by dint of the visiting two adults proving to be surprisingly grown-up, considerate, and insisting on being kitchen assistants, deputy or lead chefs on alternate days and the older children proving well-versed in the scrape and chop department as well as in other delights of the culinary world such as sorting out the recycling, washing dishes, and tidying up their bedrooms with hardly any breakages and no tears.

Hugo and Mafwaney treated the whole gathering to a few meals out and takeaways, insisting their income as, respectively, small music company co-director and orchestra violinist, could well allow for this extravagance. This certainly went against Angela's stubborn mental image of them living in squalor as struggling artists and busking musicians, born of her permanent view of her son as someone who could never quite manage his own shoelaces or cross the road unaided, despite his now being a hearty 32-year-old with children of his own. Her concerns about needing to learn to cook an extravagant range of exotic and obscure dishes to meet the dietary requirements of her Afro-Canadian daughter-in-law and grandchildren were also groundless as she found they were all accustomed to food with which she was quite familiar herself – as well as being well able to introduce her to some exotic, obscure, and quite delicious wonders which she didn't need to cook herself but could enjoy.

Tea at the maternal great-grandparents, in a distant and more diverse part of town, where they had moved to downsize when their pension plan had been stolen, had gone well – apart from one gaff where Angela's dad had asked Mafwaney what her first language was. They were surprised when she had said 'French' as their grasp of Canadian history, as well as of African diaspora, was somewhat foggy. Mafwaney had smiled and explained about Canada's languages and her own background then more cakes were eaten, tea was drunk, family photographs shared, and great-grandchildren mystified by strange anecdotes about their father's childhood antics.

A walk in the nearby park relaxed everybody,

where other multicoloured families were out together in the sunshine. On a trip to a country pub for lunch on another day, however, Angela and her parents had noticed some unfriendly stares of a kind they had not received before. Hugo noticed too and advised them to 'just ignore it – you get used to it'. Mafwaney and he would smile graciously and nod at the starers in quiet dignity, inciting confused frowns and lookings-away. Angela looked cross but followed her son's advice and the children's lead in taking no notice of other people's rudeness and ignorance. She and I may have given out such looks in the not-too-distant past, in our more ignorant days, but had never before been on their receiving end.

To avoid such anticipated 'unpleasantness' in her own neighbourhood of the well-clipped, well-heeled cul-de-sac, Angela had carefully arranged for outings to begin mid-morning and to end by mid-afternoon so that departure from and return to the cul-de-sac would not occur when its other residents were either heading towards or returning from their daily work, dog-walkings, or other leisure activities. Angela had lived there long enough to be able to produce a written timetable of who did what and when should one ever be required. Fitting in the bundling of supplies and children into cars in between Mrs Fitzsimmons's elegant walk to the newsagent to get her *Telegraph* and Mr Richardson's brisk expedition to the common with his matched pedigree pointers became something of an art form, together with avoiding the morning and afternoon cavalcades of commuting cars whisking their rested, fed and watered owners back to whichever treadmill it was upon which they earned enough to maintain a smart car and hefty mortgage. Angela also ensured that it was always one of the lighter skin toned of the four children to help her take the recycling to the pavement-side on the allotted evening in case someone was watching or happened to pass. Neither parent seemed to notice or suspect her subterfuge.

The postie and the milkie always called (apparently) in those mythical hours around dawn so they were not a problem and the recycling crew always arrived promptly just after 6 p.m. one evening a week when the entire street's inhabitants would suddenly pour across their manicured drives and front lawns, carrying bags of pink or green, to hover for a few minutes in awkward attempts at neighbourliness before retreating back into comfortable isolation – so that weekly time of busy-ness was easily avoided too.

Angela didn't really interact with her neighbours beyond the occasional chat. Some she hadn't spoken to for years since the children had grown up and stopped playing in each others' gardens. Such tenuous connections as had survived that watershed change had recently been frayed to the point of total severance by her having wantonly joined the ranks of 'single woman' and consequent threat to any respectable household by means of having had her husband leave her. She had, however, a clear idea, from previous interactions and occasional chats, that her having suddenly acquired a family of colour would not enhance her standing in the eyes of her immediate neighbours – all of whom were polite, softly spoken, and very sincere in their mourning of the passing of that 'sensible' apartheid system in South Africa.

Only twice during the visit had the family come close to an unwanted encounter: once, when a dropped ball had rolled away from its infant owner during the scramble to get into the cars for one outing to the park. It rolled under the car, down the drive, across the road, and straight down the driveway of the house opposite. Angela scampered after it like a ferret, outdistancing her junior rival in the race by a length driven, no doubt, by the fearful panic of discovery and consequent exposure. She practically dived down the slope of the neighbour's opposite driveway, setting off their dog/Hellhound/wolfpack into a frenzy of barking from behind the prettily netted windows. Fortunately, the dog or dogs did this every day at fairly regular intervals so nobody came rushing to investigate, no faces appeared at the windows to discover the surreptitious escape, no alarm was raised across the quiet street. Angela grabbed the errant football and the hand of the child, ran back up the drive, pushed it, him, the rest of us, and herself into her and my cars. We rode away unseen, Angela checking in the rear-view mirror. I saw Mafwaney looking at Angela speculatively as if she suspected the reason for this sudden burst of uncharacteristic speed but she said nothing and Hugo was oblivious. That was the first time the family came close to being discovered by our neighbours.

The children, fired by the experience of home-schooling during Lockdown and still being of the age to interact freely with others of their kind without formal introduction, asked if they could put on a puppet show and invite 'the neighbourhood', but Angela had diverted them away from this life-threatening peril by a trip to the local cinema. This had cost her a small fortune, eaten up her wine allowance for a fortnight, and given her a headache but had bought her peace of mind for an hour or two by keeping the neighbours away. Hugo had reminisced for a while about some of the friendships he had had in his childhood and speculated where they would all be now as adults. He and Angela had had a brisk discussion about which child had lived where or belonged to which set of parents in which house and whether they were still there or had moved away – it sounded like one of those puzzles where you have to work out whose house has the yellow door or owns the zebra. For Angela it was all a bit of a blur as the children had all seemed pretty much interchangeable, even at the time; living in and out of each other's gardens and houses like a multi-headed, playful amoeba moving around the cul-de-sac with Hugo's being the one face she could pick out of the crowd with any degree of certainty.

It made her tearful as she recalled days when people had visited and talked to each other, if only to pass on an invitation to the next Great Event with cake and balloons in one or other of the houses or to haul one or other child out of a garden to attend its own home for one meal or another or bed-time. The days of her young adulthood had been days of young parenthood and the cul-de-sac had been a friendlier, livelier place with all the children living there being around the same age bracket and growing up together. There had even been street parties and the road itself utilised for go-cart and ball games with lookouts posted at the lower end to shout out if cars approached from the main road over the common. Nevermore.

So Angela and I managed to keep her unconventional family (if you accepted the conventions of the close) out of sight and outrage and no burning crosses appeared on the front lawn. Fortunately, there was other scandalous material afoot to satisfy the neighbourhood's hunger for event and malice. The gossip of the day, shared with her on a milk-fetching walk to the newsagents by the greying-haired bespectacled gentleman next door, out clipping his front lawn roses, was about a group of Travellers who had pitched up on the nearby common, causing an ecstasy of speculation in the area. There had been Travellers coming to the common for as long as there had been a common, some said their sojourning there even predated the advent of its being called a 'common', the building of most of the town, all of the cul-de-sac, and the invention of cars, but this was only a rumour so fear and speculation never failed to greet this almost annual extraordinary event. Angela hoped this would serve to detract the neighbourhood enough to prevent anyone noticing her own deviation from the unspoken norms and her hidden family. The local shopkeeper had actually confided to her one day on a bread-fetching trip that he had had to be extra careful that very morning as his shop had been invaded by no fewer than four 'dark-skinned' children, 'obviously Travellers', and he 'had had to keep a sharp eye on them as we know what that lot are like, don't we?'

As her four grandchildren, on the way to the park earlier that day, had all asked to stop en route and visit the local shop with their weekly pocket money to get sweets, she had had no doubt which four children had caused such consternation in the old bigot but said nothing. Angela had stopped the car just around the corner from the shop and had sat, sweating, at the wheel, keeping a sharp eye out for any spies during the children's dangerous trip into enemy territory. She had heard Mafwaney reminding them as they had climbed out of the car to 'make sure to keep your hands in your pockets while you're in there'. She had been puzzled by this instruction after a lifetime of exhorting the young Hugo to do the complete opposite until Mafwaney had spotted her puzzled expression and explained, "It's less easy for them to be accused of shoplifting if they have their hands tucked away."

As Angela's frown had not cleared, Hugo had explained, "It's because they're black, Mum, and some people are racist – they get accused of stuff they don't do." Angela had blushed at her own ignorance of the world and at Hugo having used the 'b' word.

Angela had said nothing to correct the shopkeeper later that day. Telling me about it afterwards, she said she felt guilty for not saying anything to correct him but what else could she have done?

"I know they're my grandchildren, Beth," she had said, "but I do have to live here. If the shopkeeper found out, everyone else would know in half a minute."

I had agreed.

Angela and I had discussed what to do in the eventuality of a problem. We had decided that if any queries were raised with her, if anyone in the close did catch sight of her son's family despite all our efforts, she would pass them off with reference to the former gardener, Jake, whom she and some others in the area had sometimes employed and who had been, and probably still was, black. No-one in the close was likely to know if he had children or not – conversation about personal matters with gardeners not being 'the done thing', so if anyone had glimpsed them or Mafwaney, Angela felt she would have a good enough cover story about this gardener calling to collect some forgotten garden implement or other – she wavered between hoe and trowel – and bringing his child/children/wife (depending on who had been seen) with him. Fortunately she had only needed to use this particular piece of deception on one occasion when our immediate neighbour had called to see 'if everything was alright' as he had glimpsed 'some children who are not from the close' at the bottom of our back garden, an area visible from his upstairs window and which we had long since learned to keep out of when sunbathing and which was out of bounds to the children on the grounds that it contained 'stinging nettles'. This had worked until a badminton shuttlecock had been hit too enthusiastically and the older children had ventured gingerly into the forbidden territory, tiptoeing among the apparently invisible nettles to retrieve it – and had been spotted.

Mr Fitzimmons had been most concerned at what

he had seen from his upstairs window but had gone away after Angela's cheerful explanation on the doorstep, quite reassured that the intruders were the children of the ex-gardener who was calling on legitimate business so were only temporarily in the vicinity and were not marauding interlopers so the world as he knew it was not threatened with an untimely end. He also understood that Angela's whispered tones were due to her having a troublesome Springtime cold and her holding the door all but closed behind her was due to her not wanting to let a draught into the house as she explained the situation. He had never employed Jake himself of course, he and his wife being two of those who had expressed polite disquiet at their neighbours employing a black gardener, protesting it 'lowered the tone', but nothing had come of it and Jake had continued to make the gardens bloom until he had landed a better job in town and quit.

Angela was relieved that we had anticipated and prepared for such a sighting and that she had prepared a credible story as cover and thought no more of it.

Between smuggling children and daughter-in-law to and from the car in the drive at quiet times; herding them to play only in the well-hedged back garden with its mythical patches of nettles; pleading the traffic danger of the almost car-free road to keep them off the open-plan, front lawn, plus arranging evening outings to begin only at mealtimes and to end only after dark, Angela and my own nerves were quite worn to a frazzle. All this made my own efforts in smuggling Simon, my young lover, into and out of my B&B look quite mundane and half-hearted. The great-grandparents, Angela's mum and dad, had had no such problem at their house, showing off 'our great-grandkids' to anyone who happened to be passing when they had arrived and flagging the neighbours down to make introductions. Angela told me she was glad they had moved (downsized) years ago to the other side of town, where varying skin-tones were the norm and turned no heads whatsoever. Her parents' own attitudes had changed as well, their long-held prejudices crumbling in the face of experience.

Angela also had a few afternoons off-duty when Hugo took his family to visit his father, her ex-husband, Martin, who had moved out some months before. They all went to the nearest zoo with him and his new partner, 'Uncle Allan'. Angela knew of the planned day-trip and suffered paroxysms of anxiety in case anyone who knew her or Hugo or Martin would also be partaking in the delights of the zoological gardens that afternoon, but it all seemed to have gone off without incident apart from the youngest having dropped a dolly in the Giant Tortoise enclosure which then had to be rescued (the dolly, not the Giant Tortoises). I had taken charge of festivities, too, when

Angela had had to attend a seminar on her Film Appreciation Course. I had supervised the children, making cheese and chive scones in the kitchen with parents acting as kitchen-hands and referees amidst the unholy mess of flour and dishes into which the kitchen happily descended. The crumbly, yellowish blobs that had emerged from their efforts were delicious.

Another time we packed Hugo and Mafwaney off for an afternoon's child-free leisure-time and ran a Grand Festival of Children's Films – I had brought the first two Harry Potter films in DVD which I thought looked fun but Mafwaney had said they were really for older children so we had watched the adventures of Shrek and Fiona instead, which were quite enthralling as neither Angela nor I had ever seen a princess kick quite so much ass before or be loved without being beautiful. We all had pizza in the interval and ice cream at the end. Hugo and Mafwaney came home looking refreshed and rather tousled and nobody asked where they had been.

I occasionally snuck off to meet with Simon during the weeks of the family's visit but I had noticed that the glow had somewhat dimmed on our relationship now there was no potentially irate husband in the background and, indeed, since my realisation that said husband had never even been potentially irate but actually quite delighted as my own infidelities had merely bequeathed him time and space in which to indulge his own. I had noticed a certain lack of acute disappointment in myself when, on occasion, Simon had proved to be unavailable for a liaison – more frequently than previously as well – without considering why this might be as everything else, including his erratic zero-hour shift pattern and odd-job engagements, had remained the same.

Despite all her misgivings and fears, Angela had quite simply fallen in love with her grandchildren and found an ally and friend in her daughter-in-law, Mafwaney. Once indoors, with the curtains drawn, she could revel in the fun of being a grandma; playing hide and seek, making pancakes, trying to make waffles to her heart's content, vying with the parents for turns to tuck them in and read stories. She and Hugo got on a lot better now there were no lies between them, the maintenance of which had hampered their closeness for years.

All in all the weeks had flown by. Suddenly, there was the lift back to the airport and hugs and tears. "It was such a lovely visit," Angela gushed, hugging them all a second time. "It was so lovely to meet you and get to know you," she said to Mafwaney, hugging her again while Hugo went to unload the cases.

"Yes," smiled Mafwaney, hugging her back and looking at me over Angela's shoulder, "and I don't think anyone did spot us after all." The hug came to an awkward halt but Mafwaney's kind smile had not faltered as she noticed mine and Angela's discomfort.

There was a silence in the little group. Hugo and the children were out of earshot. I saw Angela's face fall and blush a deep red, her eyes seeking the ground, her mouth open but no words found. I felt my face also changing colour which was, it occurred to me, rather ironic.

"Hey, don't worry," said Mafwaney, taking Angela's hand and smiling at me, "I know what people can be like. Welcome to our world! It's been brilliant meeting you at last. Don't worry, I understand – it's not your fault. I know how cruel people can be, believe me I do."

They had another hug, this time tearful. "Our kids get called names," said Mafwaney, "and they don't get invited to some kids' parties. It hurts. They get told off by some teachers for stuff other kids get away with, they are becoming more aware of how it is. We stay out of some shops as they get treated like thieves – they know to stay away from some parts of town. I protect them as much as I can, so does Hugo."

Angela stared at her. It struck me too that we had hidden the children from people here but their mother could not hide them from the world and they had already been hurt in their little lives by the kind of people whom we had been trying not to upset! The thought of her beloved grandchildren being called names because of their beautiful skin, I could see, had brought tears to Angela's eyes. Mafwaney kissed her on the cheek and wiped them away, saying, "Don't worry. We all had a great time and we'd like to come again next year!"

Then the cases had to be carried, the children gathered, another hug for 'Granny Angie' and 'Aunty Beth', passports located once more, and the gates gone through until all were out of sight.

We watched the spot where they had disappeared for a long time.

Then there was the sudden empty silence of the drive home and the house was returned to the presence of just two middle-aged women, one in tears and both wondering, what next?

Chapter Two
Some Changes

Angela spent a few days grieving and wondering if she could afford a trip to Canada quite soon. One of her grandchildren had a birthday coming up with a house party planned with friends from school, games, cake, balloons, and other wonders. She agonised over what to send and not being able to be there – although a Skype call was arranged as some kind of comfort.

We quit the 'avoiding the neighbours' routine and relaxed into noisily and frequently walking out at busy times and ostentatiously bumping into our neighbours passing by for some inane chat as if to make up for lost time. Instead of rushing our recycling to the roadside and hurtling back inside, as we had been doing, we took to absolutely dawdling along and even staying to exchange comments on the weather – the nearest to actual 'chat' which was considered proper –

with the neighbourhood's other early-evening sojourners, carrying their sundry bags full of random bits of plastic, cardboard, or garden shrubbery off-cuts to the pavement-edge, as if we were all at a particularly low-budget Bring-and-Buy sale.

Of course we were both unemployed now. Angela's husband, Martin, had failed to return despite all Angela's anticipations of the contrary – his 'temporary fling ' with his new-found love, Allan, having shifted gears and moved into the slow lane of steady relationship with rumours of marriage on the horizon. A few of Angela's neighbours had been very kind, coming around with cake, possibly as delegates, and asking gently probing questions but she had let nothing slip beyond the obvious, that he had left. The cul-de-sac hadn't quite woken up to the fact that gay and bisexual people actually existed and Angela did not feel it incumbent upon herself to break the shocking news to them. With that and keeping the multi-coloured clan of Hugo's family out of neighbouring eyes, she was fast running out of corners in which to hide parts of her life.

Unfortunately for her plans for privacy, this was a small town and Martin and Allan, surprisingly, did not spend all their time locked away in their new flat but actually went out and about together, as lovers often do. We could tell exactly when they had been spotted because Mrs Fitzsimmons from next door, acting either independently or delegated by a posse, we couldn't be sure, called around on the pretence of selling raffle tickets for her church's roof repairs despite Angela and myself each having already bought ten. The conversation hurtled towards the recent sighting, apparently at a café, and politely smiling questions about who 'the other gentleman' might be. Heartily tired of keeping secrets Angela gave our visitor a brief outline of the case and the politely shocked Mrs Fitzsimmons left very soon afterwards with the same satisfied smile on her face as you'd expect to see on that of a sated vulture rising from the carcass of a freshly dead antelope. We knew the scandalous story would be around the close within the hour.

Our social lives had already shrunk somewhat: as single women we were, of course, quietly dropped from dinner party invitations and other gatherings, even in between lockdowns. We had quit the Golf Club, feeling the normal icy chill of polite welcome becoming icier. Again, as single women we were now seen as predatory and a possible threat to husbands' fidelity. This was normal and part of the social circle in which we had, if not exactly whirled then at least strolled, since the dawn of time and these were views which we had held ourselves and colluded in to the exclusion of others who had fallen by the wayside by clumsy means of divorce or widowhood. 'Single women were not welcome and they were out to get your husband' was the accepted understanding. We hadn't noticed before that this view was most strongly held by those who seem to have not recently taken a good look at their husbands.

The company for which Angela and Martin had both worked had, after all, gone into 'downsize', using the pandemic as an excuse, like so many others, to lay off half the staff to get the remainder to work twice as fast at half the cost and Angela had been laid off. My own estate agency company which my father had built and left to me had foundered at last, half the population having lost interest in buying houses and the other half in selling them. I had 'gone bust' as the saying goes, I believe. I had shut up shop for the time-being. I was alright: the capital from the sale to a much more well-founded company would see me through but I'd had to 'let staff go' of course to make the sale so I hadn't made any friends in the town. Fortunately, my wayward husband and my equally wayward self had then eyed each other warily across the divorce battlefield, crossed as it was with coils of barbed wire laid by our various solicitors, and, to their great and several disappointments, reached an agreement where we could both survive – renting out and sharing the funds from the family home with its swimming pool – and staying clear of court. There were broken hearts among the soliciting fraternity that day I can tell you, or, at least, given the lack of the required organ in said grouping, there were weeping wallets.

Angela and I had both fallen from our comfort zone but it looked as though we would not be falling far. I paid her rent – having returned to my room when the family left – and we shared the bills, an arrangement which kept us both afloat. The funds from renting out the house kept me in clean knickers and my rent to Angela helped her along but we needed to think of something by which we could earn more as we did not intend to live austerely – indeed neither of us would know how. Martin had insisted on paying an amount from his income as a psychiatrist into their still valid joint account for her use but she would not touch it.

"How can I accept anything from him?" she had asked. "I'm too angry!" I suggested that being angry was fine but there *were* other ways to express anger which still got the bills paid and proposed a few, some involving pins and dolls while others included knives and tyres or anchovies hidden inside curtain rails to decompose or involving severed brake cables, but it was too soon for her to pay attention to good advice.

Angela's case was similar to mine: as a homeowner she could not claim any support from the state and the rent I paid would not keep her in petrol, wine, coffee, or her online college fees, nor would her savings last very long, not in the way she wanted to live anyway. We had to make plans.

Seeing a rare 'for sale' notice up on a house in the close some weeks previously had given me an idea. An ad in the paper, advertising for small-business advice, gave Angela another.

"I'll bet there are loads of people wanting to know how much their home is worth and looking for ideas to make it worth more – they need someone like me!" I calculated, my estate agent's instincts for a fast (and easy) buck kicking in.

"And I know all about running a business already from training courses at HR. I bet there are loads of self-employed types and small businesses drowning in paperwork and employment law, needing someone like me to help them wade though it all!"

We got cards and flyers made, Hugo was recruited and his artistic and publicity talents put to good use, sending us bespoke advertising gems from across the Atlantic to print off. We had the idea of not using our own names on the flyers, just in case, and Hugo made the appropriate adaptations. Angela's was more like a flyer and my own was a smaller, smart-looking card – they each included our mobile numbers on them, stating that our 'relevant qualifications could be perused on request', which was true. We both had drawers full of certificates from down the years, some of them yellowing and actually curling at the edges like old sandwiches but they added up to an impressive array of bits of paper and scraps of knowledge. We used our original surnames to put any local nosey-parkers off the scent with totally invented first names to deceive anyone more local who might know us and chose eye-catching but sophisticated logos to decorate our publicity. We offered a good third off the going rate for house evaluations, marketing, legal or employment advice, and for bespoke book-keeping.

In the early hours of several mornings we delivered our ads. We began with the immediate neighbours, reasoning that anyone wanting to use our services instead of those of an office in town of an established, some would say legitimate, company would also want to keep as quiet about it as we did so there was no reason not to include them. I also included some of Simon's cards in the bundles which we dropped through letter boxes – he usually worked for an agency but the work was erratic and badly paid so he broke his zero-hour contract by 'moonlighting' when he could. His working hours had often meant our times for liaison on a more personal level were also erratic and irregular. That had always added to the frisson of the affair. Now it was just tiresomely inconvenient.

All went well with posting the cards and flyers: the

close was quiet and sleepy in the grey light as we flitted from driveway to driveway, except for the house opposite, of course, where all Hell got raised the moment my errant foot stepped across from the tarmac of the pavement to the Golden Gravel of the sacred territory and continued until I had once more regained the pavement. I felt an unfamiliar solidarity with posties and milkies and the risks they ran.

For several days, if the weather was dry, we would drive around this or one of the other 'moneyed' parts of town, park the car, and 'do' several streets at once, pushing the cards and leaflets through each letter box – sometimes encountering snarls or barks from within but otherwise seeing no signs of life and never actually losing a limb.

People responded. We had a slow but steady trickle of people wanting their books sorted or seeking advice about enhancing their house's market value – cash in hand and no questions asked. We felt we had turned a corner. Life, with good wine and coffee, could go on, which, after all, was the only life either of us could face at all with equanimity. It was bending a few tax laws, maybe, but needs must.

It was a few weeks after the family's departure that the complications began.

It was in early March and the night of the little one's birthday party in Canada. Angela had

27

discovered that the time-lapse between here and the outskirts of Vancouver was about seven hours so, if she wanted to join the party and have a brief chat with her beloved grandchildren, wish the one 'happy birthday', and join in the singing when they brought the cake out, she would need to ring when it was six thirty over there and …

"1.30 in the morning?" I exclaimed, knowing Angela, job or no job, was not one for burning the candle at either end any more than I was when not romantically occupied.

"It'll be fine," she said, "I'll set my alarm. Can I borrow your Skype again?"

This request was a bit redundant as, since her initiation into the wonders of Skype, my computer had been more or less permanently ensconced in her room at the front of the house – my interactions with my own family's international diaspora having become less and less frequent as children and grandchildren had aged and grown further away than had anything to do with geography.

"And you come too, they loved you! 'Auntie Beth'," she insisted.

I had to admit that I had enjoyed my new role as surrogate auntie.

So Angela bought party hats and various things that make a party-like noise and in the evening set her alarm clock. As it happened we just stayed up, watching one of her beloved old films, drinking coffee and wine until the awaited hour.

People have always travelled around this lonely globe which we call home looking for safety or for the chance to work, to contribute, looking for a home, a sense of belonging, to be with family or friends, to be safe, to get away from the ravages and horrors of war, famine, climate catastrophe or all three, but I think Hugo mostly went to Canada to get away from Angela.

Not only Angela of course but his dad, Martin, as well and the life they had both mapped out for him. They had wanted him to be a psychiatrist, a barrister, or a doctor but he, inconveniently, had wanted to make music and art. A friend had opened that door for him and he had flit – all the way to Canada. Angela and Martin had blamed the economy, each other, and the ridiculous emigration rules which allowed this but really they could only blame themselves. They had not been able to accept the child they'd had, so he had gone.

Skype of course had abbreviated the miles apart for many and brought people closer together but Hugo had said for years that he could not work 'the horrible machine' and had kept to the limits of telephone and letter to communicate with his parents in between his solo visits. The reason for this was apparent now: he had been able to keep up the pretence of his 'wild, single life' which he'd related to Angela in telephonic episodes and hide the fact that he was actually happily married – only because the telephone does not disclose the giveaway trappings of domesticity, such as a wife and four children in the background. Now the truth was out and the phone calls could be replaced by online gatherings with updates and news, which were much more mundane and happier than his previous fabricated listings of nightclub outings and wild, romantic entanglements. Hugo had kept the secret of his interracial marriage a secret until his father's own secret about his sexuality was disclosed, which had rather trumped it and the seismic changes this had caused in the family geology had allowed the light through and for Hugo to also begin to be honest about who he was and where life had brought him.

Angela missed her grandchildren. I had suggested that maybe, as she now had to stop living vicariously through Hugo's supposed wild single life of romantic adventure, she should trip the light fantastic herself, now and again, having shed the grey ensemble of domestic bliss. As her husband had sloughed off with his lover, it left space for other possibilities to grow in her life but she had only got as far as turning her hobby of film-watching into an online course of Film Appreciation and ditching her Golf Club membership.

Losing her job, her husband, as well as delusions in her son and her best friend (my long-term infidelity, if it's still called that, having come as another recent shock to her) were probably a big enough set of changes in her life for the time being, as well as launching away from routine respectable employment into a life of precarious self-employment and tax-dodging.

"Besides," she had said, "how can I ever trust anyone again?"

She had also had to quit being racist. Or to start to quit: years of indoctrination and accepting wider society's unspoken norms as Truth for decades not, after all, being wipe-off-able with a damp cloth overnight. Her parents had already managed much of this journey, prompted by brushes with their own mortality, fatal illness, helpful neighbours, and hospital staff of quite a spectrum of skin tones, origins, and religions. Long-held beliefs and superstitions cracked and fell under the weight of actual experience. Ignorance was at last displaced. They had even switched newspapers.

In their earlier lives Angela's parents, like all good, respectable racists, had subtly taught Angela that certain children at school were not to be invited to birthday parties nor similar invitations accepted. They had educated her about which people on the television were inferior, having been taught this themselves in lessons about the British Empire and

31

the need for white people to take charge at gunpoint if necessary in order to save the world. To have found, later in life, that this was all hogwash was something of a shock if not a disappointment but also something of a relief as they could now be friends with people they actually liked and not choose acquaintanceships by use of a colour chart. Their social lives and mental health had improved accordingly but the cocoon of work and Golf Club had thus far insulated Angela and myself against any such threat of personal growth and discovery.

Angela, long insulated from much of the reality of life by robust health and a good income, had not thought about the many assumptions with which she had been brought up until her grandchildren and daughter-in-law had turned up, black and beautiful. Experience trumps bigotry.

I had also had to unpack some dusty baggage and throw out some ancient, moth-eaten idiocies from forgotten corners of my mind to let in the sun and air which showed the world to be quite different than it had appeared from behind multiple shades of ignorance and bigotry's dusty, comfortable cobwebs.

Of course, letting the neighbours or the Golf Club set know of these transformations, however partial, wasn't an option so our memberships were allowed to lapse. We didn't talk about it, we just stopped going there, but moving house is a bit trickier than cancelling subs. We had successfully kept Hugo's family out of the sight of neighbours during their visit and I was careful that my young lover, Simon, who, although of the right skin-shade, was certainly not of the right social class, only ever visited the house after dark with his high-vis yellow vest well tucked away in an inside pocket so, with respectability intact, life could go on. Our change in employment status from salaried HR officer and Estate Agent, respectively, to 'self-employed' tax-evaders on the edges of the economy was also well hidden. We had eventually switched supermarkets, of course, but this was also not discernible as we were careful to only go shopping at night.

The night of the 15th, a Monday, was the birthday party night.

Chapter Three

An Incident

The film Angela was currently studying did a pretty good job of keeping us awake, ironically, until the allotted time, although the red wine did a brave battle in the other direction. I mean, who wouldn't stay awake for Humphrey Bogart in a snap-brim fedora? Angela made some notes for her course in between sips of wine.

"Have all the films you study got to be ancient?" I asked as *The Big Sleep* rolled to its conclusion at about 1 a.m. and our self-imposed insomnia began to hit home with wine-tinted, grey clouds rolling in softly across our conscious minds.

"No," said Angela, enthusiastically, the subject being films, "the next project on the course is to study one old – at least 50 years old – film and compare the 'narrative devices' with a 'very recent film of our own choice' and do a presentation online," she explained, rubbing her eyes. "Coffee?"

"God yes!" I said. "What's a narrative device?" I asked, trying desperately to care but before I had an answer the alarm went off and the party was on.

I turned on the lights and Angela got the Skype working.

The party in Canada was in full and manic swing with face-painted juveniles giggling into the camera, hundreds of miles away, shouting hellos and showing us an assortment of toys while we waved, questioned, listened, and wished. Angela wanted to read them a funny story and I left her to it out of respect to a grandma's prerogatives. Angela had the heating on in her room so I found it too warm and stuffy. I went over to the window and opened it. My old enemy, the orange streetlight, lit up the road and the front lawn but no other lights were on in the sleeping close that I could see. I leant on the sill to get some air. Angela was reading the story to the screen which flickered grey in the darkened room. A child in Canada occasionally piped up a question but all else was quiet. I saw a large, flat-faced bird – I guessed it had to be an owl at this time of night – swoop by on its silent wings, palest orange in the light from the street lamp, and disappear into the navy blue darkness.

Then, as I leaned on the sill in the cool March air, a

car came revving up the hill from the main road, the beams from its headlights swinging into the cul-de-sac. A light-beige car with a pale orange roof, the driver having difficulty with the gears and the sloping road, drove quite quickly into view then stopped in front of the house opposite. There was a young man in the driving seat. I could see his short sideburns and glasses.

I heard the passenger-side door open and a woman with long dark hair and a bright red coat got out of the car. I heard her high heels hit on the tarmac of the road and pavement then crunch onto gravel as she ran down the driveway opposite, past the two cars which were parked in it. She was holding a square of white, which I took to be paper, in one hand which she held aloft as if to help her keep balance as she went awkwardly down the drive. I remembered the agony of high-heels in my own youth, especially on gravel, and felt a pang of sympathy. Her form quickly became a silhouette in the half-light. She moved down the drive to the front door of the house opposite then ducked down for a moment, out of sight, as if tying a shoelace. When she straightened up she didn't turn to go back up the drive as I expected but instead I saw her shadowy figure step off to the left side of the house, disappearing around the corner.

Curious, I waited for what would happen next. Whoever was driving the car didn't switch off the engine. There was a pause. The car engine thrummed gently in the night air. My old friend the owl shrieked some distance away, another hooted soulfully. A couple of minutes passed. Then the woman came back out of the shadows of the side of the house and up the driveway into the streetlight's circle of light once more. She was panting as if she had been running for miles and was stooped, the coat collar obscuring most of her face. As she came to the top of the drive I could see that she seemed to be wearing a white skirt or trousers under the red coat.

She opened the back door of the car as if she was getting in there but then, seeming to change her mind, closed the back door again and got back into the front seat. The driver glanced over his right shoulder before pulling off and I briefly saw a pale, round face with glasses and short, light hair. The car drove off quickly, even before the passenger could have had time to put her seatbelt on. The car headed up the close and disappeared. I imagined it doing a u-turn in the little circular patch at the top of the road which was for this very purpose, but not usually at this hour of the night. Then it came back into view and drove past again. A face looked up at me momentarily from the passenger seat as the car passed, she and I both lit momentarily by the streetlight, then quickly sped away. I got an impression of a young, heart-shaped face with a lot of dark hair with a fringe and an Alice band. The beige car disappeared towards the main road. Something about the car looked familiar.

"That's odd," I thought.

Behind me, the Skype call was continuing and I went to be 'Auntie Beth' again. We played 'Skype Hide and Seek' and some I-Spy but then it was coming to an end with goodbyes and blown kisses, accepting gracious thanks from the parents for the presents we had sent, too many and far too expensive, and waves and smiles from my unofficial family.

Angela had a few tears when it was over but was smiling as well.

I closed the window, noticing that all was quiet once more outside, and drew the curtains. We finished the wine, reminisced on the party's highlights for a while, then said our goodnights.

The next day, after lunchtime, I was driving home after a whole morning selling advice to anxious home-owners about how to sell their truly awful houses to an unsuspecting and gullible public which was how I supplemented my income these days. Turning into the close I noticed paper posters had been stuck on all the lamp-posts and telegraph poles along the main road across the common and into the close. They were even stuck on trees. From what I could make out as I drove past they featured a white dog. There was one fixed on 'our' streetlight and I went to inspect it. It showed a picture of a medium-sized, fluffy white dog, standing tall on the end of a lead, in profile, with a rosette and a silver cup in full view. MISSING. HAVE YOU SEEN THIS DOG? was written in large letters, a name with contact details filled the rest of the space on the paper. There was another dog poster on our hall table. I picked it up and went to fetch a coffee.

"It's the dog across the road – the Harrisons – they breed them. They were putting these leaflets around the close. Very strange. Thieves broke in last night and stole her! Mrs Harrison is beside herself, she called round all the houses in the close to give them a poster and she's gone to the police. The Harrisons photocopied the posters this morning and put them up. Pedigree dog, worth thousands," Angela told me, in between typing paragraphs in a composition which looked like it might be about 'narrative devices' though I couldn't be sure.

"Last night?" I remembered the party and the cake in the shape of a giant strawberry that had looked so delicious and fattening and so very far away.

"Yes, they were fast asleep. This morning the dog was gone."

I gaped at her, remembering something else from the night.

"Angie, I saw something last night, I think I saw it happen!"

"Did you?" She didn't look up from her writing. "Of course she knows who did it – she knows it's the Travellers on the common, it's exactly the sort of thing they do, she said! You saw them?"

She turned and gaped at me. Sound waves do sometimes travel slowly, I'd noticed.

"Yes!" I told the tale about the beige car and the stranger in the red coat.

"If you saw something we need to go and tell her – it's a clue!"

This was exciting, I realised.

"I'll get my jacket."

I wiped off the biscuit crumbs and gulped the dregs. Together we left the house and walked down the driveway. Parked across the top of the driveway opposite was a police car – all orange stripes and blue light. We rang the bell, feeling the importance of being Bearers of Great News.

Mrs Harrison answered the door. The small pane of glass in their front door was mostly missing and some black and yellow tape had been stuck around it. Some broken shards of glass were still protruding haphazardly around the edges of the hole. Angela introduced me as a 'friend who's staying for a while'. Mrs Harrison told us that it was 'not a good time for a visit' but we said, "It's about the missing dog," and were ushered inside.

In the front room a large policeman in a large uniform, who reminded me of PC Plum off the telly, was sitting with a notebook and pencil. He, and a man whom I took to be Mr Harrison, looked at us as we entered. Angela, Mrs Harrison, and he did some polite, mutual reminding of who each was and of how long it had been since they had met until the policeman coughed.

I noticed that the room was decorated with photographs of Mr and Mrs Harrison and a large white dog, or it might have been several large white dogs, wearing rosettes of various colours, together with some large trophy cups with ribbons on them. We sat down.

The policeman was looking at us. Mrs Harrison began introducing us to the policeman but Angela interrupted.

"Oh we don't need to be so formal! I'm Angela, from across the road," she explained happily to the policeman. "Our two sons," she nodded to the Harrisons, "were great pals when they were little, weren't they? Happy days – playing together with the other children in the close! Years go by so quickly, don't they?" Angela's eyes were bright as she again recalled Hugo's much-edited infancy.

There was a silence. I could have guessed her mistake. Any glance around the room at the photographs could have told her that no child had ever lived here, only dogs and the two people in front of us who were now looking slightly bemused.

Then Mr Harrison smiled awkwardly and said, "You're mixing us up with somebody, dear, we don't have a son." He said it quite gently, as if talking to someone who has been very ill and is still quite fragile. Angela blushed as she realised she had mixed up her memories again. The policeman looked us both up and down. He looked unimpressed.

Angela looked confused and blushed once more. Then we all agreed it was 'easily done' as 'all the children played all over the close in those days – in and out of each others' gardens – hard to know whose was which' reminisced Angela, with the Harrisons nodding in close formation and patient agreement.

The policeman watched this interchange. He looked at Angela and I saw her through his eyes: a middle-aged, rather flaky woman with memory problems already setting in. He glanced my way and, by his expression, I realised he saw a similar entity when he looked at me.

He marked the end of our neighbourly confusion with another cough. "Well anyway …?" he said, and we all remembered why we were there.

"My friend, Beth, saw something last night which might help," Angela announced and I was the centre of attention, even though the policeman's expression said very clearly that he very much doubted it.

I told my little tale and the policeman made notes.

"Pale beige you say? How could you be sure if it was pitch black? There was no moon last night," he added authoritatively, as one who has looked things up and knew when there were moons and when there were not.

"The street light," I explained, and pointed. He checked through the window and nodded.

"I see. You get the registration number?" He made another note. I shook my head. He grimaced, as if his worldly burden was that much heavier because of people like me who looked at cars yet failed to note their registration numbers.

"What make was it?" was the next question and it drew another blank from me.

"It was a very old car," I said, trying to be helpful.

"And they broke the window on the front door, you say?" He turned to the Harrisons, now Charles and Joan, who nodded.

"Yes, that's how they got in," said Joan, nodding.

"But you didn't hear it breaking? They must have used brown paper and glue or treacle to make it quiet, that's an old trick," Plum stated, like one who has studied front doors and knows about brown paper and old tricks.

"I thought I heard something," chipped in Charles, "but I thought it was the wind."

"And what time was that?" said the copper, pen poised.

I interrupted, "Oh, she didn't go to the front door, well, she did, but then she went down the side of the house."

The PC frowned at me. "You must be mistaken. Point of entry was the front door. Glass broken so they could reach in and turn the door knob." He read from his notes as one who would tolerate no dissent from underlings. I hesitated. Yes, it had been dark and lights can play tricks on your eyes and the angles were odd, given the slope in the drive. I couldn't be sure. Charles and Joan had nodded in unison, yes, I must be mistaken.

"I don't know what time it was," continued Charles, "I was half asleep."

"An old car, you say?" said officer Plum. "Always working on old cars, the Gypsies," he said. "An old car. Yes, sounds like Travellers to me," he said comfortably to the Harrisons, as one who had studied cars and knew all about who drove which or worked on what. He closed his notebook and stood up to leave.

"Red coat and lots of dark hair, you say? Of course

it might have been a wig. Good at disguise these people …"

"I don't mean 'old' like that," I wavered uncertainly, trying to explain.

What was the word I was looking for? I hunted for it but it eluded me.

He looked at me again, waiting for clarification of what it was I meant but when I could provide none he turned away and said, "Have you seen any strange person or persons in the vicinity recently?" he asked us all. "Anyone who might have been 'casing the joint', as we call it?"

Joan piped up excitedly, raising her hand as if she was in school. The policeman turned to her.

"The newsagent told me," Joan flustered excitedly, "he'd seen some suspicious looking children in his shop last week or so. He thought they were shoplifting but he didn't catch them at it. A whole gang of them! Dark skinned, he said they were. It must have been those Travellers!"

I saw Angela flush red and she opened her mouth but she didn't say anything, she just glared at Joan.

Charles chipped in. "It's those Travellers, isn't it? We're all thinking it so I might as well say it! They could easily come down here from the common in the night.. You know what they're like."

The policeman nodded sagely as one who knew what everybody was like.

"And how much would you say the animal in question is worth approximately?"

"Like I said, £20,000," said Joan without a pause.

The policeman's eyebrows twitched slightly.

"She's a pedigree and she's pregnant. The scan said six puppies," Joan continued, as if she had noticed the twitch, "£1,000 each at least. It cost a £1,000 to have her sired and—"

The PC raised his hands as if to indicate he already knew quite enough about how much pregnant pedigree dogs were worth and the costs of having them sired and wished to know no more.

"There haven't been any dog thefts in the area before – none reported," he said authoritatively. "How long have they been there, the Gypsies?"

"They come every year," I said, I wasn't sure why this was relevant. "Were there any dog thefts last year?"

The policeman looked at me and then away, "I'll enquire."

He headed to the door and we all traipsed after him like disciples.

"Aren't you going to dust it for fingerprints?"asked Angela, looking at the broken window.

"I don't think so, Madam, these professionals wear gloves. I think I'll be visiting our friends on the common."

"I don't think she was wearing gloves," I said uncertainly, but I don't think anyone heard me.

We all filed out into the drive. Some glass crunched under my shoes on the drive. There seemed to be quite a rush hour of people in the close just then – walking past with their dogs or alone, being careful not to be seen to look at the police car, the policeman getting into it, or at us.

The policeman left with his notebook. Charles and Joan said how nice it was to see Angela again, how nice it was to meet me and how they mustn't leave it so long next time but no coffee was offered nor biccies and we were ushered gently away with many pleasantries and vague invitations.

"Coffee and a biccie?" said Angie as we got in.

"Ooh yes, go on."

"Was she wearing gloves? The woman last night?" she asked.

I thought for a minute. "I don't think so. She was too far away … mind you, she was on the other side of the road."

"Did you hear her knock the window out?"

"Don't think so. But I thought she went down the

47

side of the house so what do I know? Light and shadows play tricks at night and my eyesight's not what it was."

"Oh well, no doubt the police will sort it out. You seeing Simon tonight?"

"No, cancelled again. Beginning to wonder if he hasn't got someone else hidden away."

"Well you've always had somebody else hidden away – your husband, Frank."

"That's different!"

"Didn't Simon ask you to leave said husband to be with him?"

"That's also different."

"But isn't it—?"

"Look, it's all different, okay?"

"Worried?"

"Not sure. More relieved really, thinking about it. It's quite hard work making myself glamorous for a hot date. It's nice to just get in my housecoat and jammies and put my feet up."

"Wine?"

"Yup, that too." We filled our glasses.

The report was in the local paper that evening, if you looked hard enough. Just a small paragraph which you wouldn't see unless you were looking for it:

'Pedigree Dog theft - Police Investigating.'

We spent the evening wallpapering Hugo's old room with a paper he and Mafwaney had chosen. We were drinking wine and chewing over the details of Angela's essay on *The Big Sleep* and its 'narrative devices' as we slapped on the glue and wallpaper. Two of the rolls of paper went on upside down but somehow it worked and the essay seemed more and more hilarious as the level in the bottle fell.

It seemed that was that and our little brush with adventure and the Underworld was over.

The following morning there was a bigger report all over the front page: 'Theft of Precious Dog; Gypsy Arrested'.

There was a photo of Joan and Charles and their fluffy white champion dog with its ridiculous four-barrelled name on one side of the article and, on the other, a photo of the caravans on the common with an inserted photo of a thin-faced young man with dreadlocks and a youthful effort at a beard and moustache looking wide-eyed at the camera. There was a quote in heavy print from Charles saying how the dog was a much-loved family pet and that they were 'heartbroken'.

"It was a woman I saw though," I said, eyeing the photograph of the young man, trying to remember what the young man in the driver's seat had looked like and thinking he hadn't had dreadlocks.

"Probably a whole gang of them," said Angela, pouring coffee. "Biccie?"

But there were other developments too.

Among the morning's offerings of brown envelopes and catalogues offering more convenient ways of life with numerous gadgets and devices which together could make a very inconvenient and expensive mountain in anyone's home, there was a photocopy of a handwritten flyer done in black felt pen. It was succinct and to the point if somewhat lacking in subtle elegance: 'No To Gypsy Camp', it said, then, in smaller writing, 'Public meeting for all citizens concerned about law and order' in the local Scout Hut meeting room on the coming Thursday evening. Apparently all were welcome.

"Do you think we should go?" said Angela around a mouthful of ginger nuts.

"Nah, we've done enough, besides I've got three reports of recommendations on three different houses I need to write up and I keep mixing up the one with dry rot and the one with woodworm with the one that has a subsiding wall and rising damp."

"And I've got to finish that project on narrative devices *and* watch a brand new film to 'compare and contrast' with the older one."

"Have you found a brand new film? I was beginning to think they don't make them anymore."

"Yes!" Angie replied, ignoring the sarcasm. "It's just been made, it's based on a book – title from an old Sherlock Holmes story or something, *The Curious Incident of the Dog in the Night-Time*. Brilliant, apparently – won awards and things."

"Was that the dog on the moor, frightening people to death?"

"No, that was the Baskervilles' one. All this dog did was it didn't bark when it should have done and only Sherlock spotted the significance and that was the clue."

We reached for our glasses of wine then stopped at the same moment and looked at each other wide-eyed with sudden realisation.

"It didn't bark!"

Chapter Four

Encounters

I'd been in the Scout Hall on precisely one previous occasion and the idea of repeating the experience made the idea of sticking pins in my eyes seem like a really good plan for the forthcoming evening's entertainment and I said so. Angela, however, was entranced:

'We must go – we must be part of this community. Crime is all our problem!"

She did watch rather a lot of public warning advertisements together with re-runs of: *Columbo, Frost, Poirot, Midsomer Murders, Bergerac, The Sweeney, Morse, Lewis, Maigret, Foyle's War, NYPD Blue, Dixon of Dock Green, Rosemary and Thyme, Cagney and Lacey, Heartbeat, The Professionals, Z-cars, Starsky and Hutch, Shaft,* and *The Champions,* all of which crowded the airways with images of astute, intrepid, and scrupulously honest heroes tracking down the errant evildoers in our midst.

I conceded, trying to eradicate memories of dusty exercise mats and exhortations from a twenty-something health fanatic to stretch and pull and heave, as if I was not an elegant fifty-something in search of a little moderate toning but a reluctant and rather drunken press-gang victim to His Majesty's Navy out on swabbing duty. Coffee would not suffice so I planned to raid the brandy cupboard and fill a small elegant flask with the necessary.

"What do you think it's about? Something to do with the dog being stolen?"

"Could be."

"Oh come on, we should go. It'll be a change, we could meet some people …?"

"Well you go then, I've met people before."

We speculated for a while over breakfast. We were neither of us aware of any rising tide of shoplifting in the local overpriced sweetshop/garage/supermarket upon which everyone in the immediate area without a car or inclination for wider foraging depended for sustenance and printed information, although the guy who owned it needed watching in terms of handing back incorrect change and pressing the wrong buttons on the card charger.

To our knowledge there had been no murders of note: the theft of the dog over the road remained our one brush with the desperate underworld, apart from the outraged reports about people caught fiendishly working while on benefits which were the staple diet for readers of the 'Gazette', the local offering to the literary world of printed paper and frightening headlines.

The doorbell rang. Angela was expecting Martin, her departed husband, to call as she had agreed to 'having a talk'.

"I expect he'll want me to sell the house so he can claim his half," Angela had muttered bitterly into her coffee mug on reading his request. "Well, he's had that! Either that or him and Allan have split up and he wants to come creeping back!"

"Would you want him back?" I'd asked, out of curiosity. Also, if so, it would mean I'd have to make new living arrangements or get used to living in quite crowded conditions which is not 'me' at all.

Angie had frowned and hesitated. "Actually, no. If you'd asked me that a while ago I would have been desperate to get him back but now I think what a god-awful marriage it was. We did nothing together, couldn't communicate, shared nothing in common, didn't understand each other's jokes even. I'm glad he's gone actually. I've had more fun on my own. Allan's welcome to him!"

"Oh good," I said. "You're moving on. Now you can find someone better for you."

"But I'll never trust anyone again, how can I? He lied to me – for years!"

"Well, marriages often do end and there's usually quite a bit of lying involved," I offered, thinking of my own expertise in this area.

"That's different."

I didn't see how but I'd let it drop and now the day had arrived and the doorbell rang again. I had agreed to stay with Angela during the visit 'in case it got awkward'. I couldn't imagine a scenario less likely not to be quite a bit awkward from start to finish but agreed to stay and went to open the front door, picking up a newspaper which had arrived on the mat.

"Oh hello, Beth. I heard you'd moved in. How are you?"

He had parked his car in the road, I noticed, not pulled into the drive which I thought was a nice touch of sensitivity in not marking his territory in Angela's home any more. He looked like Martin but a slightly newer and improved Martin: his shirt was perhaps rather brighter and more casual than was absolutely necessary for a Thursday morning in suburbia and the moustache did nothing for him but he had lost some weight, which suited him, plus there was a sparkle in his eyes and an energy about him which had always been lacking before. He had lost some of his blandness.

"I'm fine, come in, Angela's in the kitchen."

He came in. I was pleased to see that he looked nervous and watchful. He followed me down the hall into the kitchen.

He and Angela nodded at each other and said each other's names in acknowledgement of each others' continued existence – then there was a bit of a pause.

"Coffee?" I offered, leaping into the silence like a warrior, brandishing mug and spoon.

"Please," said Martin, swallowing and, hesitatingly, sitting down on the chair Angela had pushed towards him with her foot, as if he half-expected it to collapse under him. Suddenly the room was full of the years they had spent together, or at least alongside each other, and the many breakfasts they had eaten in these four walls, mostly in silence, but also where Hugo had been rushed off to school each morning and where jigsaws and cakes had materialised on the table now between them.

Angela didn't say anything more but kept watch on him over her coffee mug as he occasionally made eye contact.

"Well," he began, "thank you for inviting me. This isn't easy—"

"I've been through worse," Angela interjected, her eyebrows raised. She had been in pieces when he had left.

Martin cleared his throat and shifted in his chair a little. "Yes," he said.

"You're not getting the house," said Angela, more loudly. "You've taken years of my life – you're not getting the house!"

He looked surprised. "I didn't ... I don't ... I'm not ... That's not why I'm here!"

"And you needn't think you're coming back either," she continued. "It was a lousy marriage and I'm glad it's over!"

I don't think she had expected to say that and she looked somewhat surprised that she had but Truth will out, some say.

Martin looked put out. "Oh come on, it wasn't all bad. I fell for you hook, line and sinker. We had some good times, we had Hugo, we had good holidays ... yes, we grew apart and it was only a matter of time before one of us—"

"Went looking for somebody else?"

"I wasn't looking – it just happened! And I thought it wouldn't ..."

This was true. From what I remembered, Martin had met Allan at a work's Suduko evening not some racy nightclub for wayward spouses.

"Yes, well it did. And I don't want you back."

"That isn't why I'm here either," he hesitated, glanced in my direction, his hands fidgeting with the coffee mug, "I loved you, Angela, I did. I've always been attracted to men but I thought it was just a phase, we were told that in those days. You met my dad and my mum, you know how they saw things. I just ignored those feelings, I hoped they'd go away. They did for a while, you and me both made that marriage work, but yes we grew apart and when I met Allan … it's not just about … you know … is it? It's who you want to be with, it's about who you really are … who I am … and I'm sorry. Me lying to myself—"

"So why *are* you here?" she snapped, pulling him up short. "You're not after the house and you're not after coming back. Good. What is it you *do* want?"

"More coffee?" I said. "Oh look, the biccies have melted." I forced a light-hearted laugh.

He took a breath, "Two things to ask you: they are connected. I don't know if you saw in the paper but my father died, a week ago …"

Angela and I both said we were sorry. I had never met the man but Angela looked genuinely taken aback and sorrowful and asked for more details about when and how and so on and if it had been peaceful.

"It wasn't a heart attack, was it, when you told him about you and Allan?" she said, which I felt was a little callous but she meant it as a genuine question. She had known the man after all.

Martin shook his head. "I never told him, I've not told anyone in my family, not my mother, not anyone."

Shocked at this I said, "You let him die without knowing his own son?"

He looked at me and I could see sadness in his eyes. "I let him die in peace. I thought it was best. You didn't know him."

Angela clued me in, "He was always going on about 'pouffs and queers' and how he hated them and how he wouldn't want any one in his family …"

There was a pause.

"Anyway," he went on, "there's the funeral next week and the whole family will be there. We – me and Allan – were going to go together, use it as a chance for me to 'come out' to the family, then let whoever can't cope with that do what they like."

"Allan and I," I couldn't help saying, correcting his grammar.

"But then," he went on, glancing at me, "Allan pointed out that my dad was your father-in-law for years and you'd probably like to come to the funeral and what would that be like for you? So, I've come to ask you."

Angela thought for a moment. I could see she appreciated being consulted and invited and so on.

She hadn't mentioned Martin's family at all so I had no idea what her relationship with them was like. 'Thin' was my guess. Still, she had been their daughter-in-law for decades.

"You mean if I came to the funeral – with you with Allan 'coming out' to everyone there – that would be difficult for me?"

"Yes."

I could see his point, everyone gossiping, Angela the 'jilted one' alone and vulnerable, what had she done to make him go 'that way' etc with everyone reeling and reacting (probably badly) to Martin and Allan's presence while his father's coffin sat neglected in the corner, forgotten among the scandal and finger buffet. Not a good funeral really, although, perhaps, a more memorable one than most?

"Yes, I think it would be," she said.

"It is my dad's funeral and I do want Allan there with me if possible but you were my best friend and my love – for years – and my dad liked you. He'd want you there too but maybe we could do the coming out part some other time if you wanted to come. Allan could just be 'a friend' and you and I just smile and wave? We weren't going to announce anything, that would be crass, just be there together, but that's no good if it excludes you. I can't sort it out so I wanted to ask you."

At least he was being thoughtful. I saw a way forward.

"What if Angela wasn't there on her own? What if she was there with someone rather handsome, better looking than you anyway, Martin. That would swing the balance a little? Then you'll have just split up with no-one being the jilted one to be pointed out and pitied?"

They both liked the idea I could tell and my little joke let them smile, albeit awkwardly.

Angela looked at me quizzically. I could see she wanted to point out there wasn't any such person but this was not the time to tell her ex-husband that there was no romance in her life so I swiftly changed the subject.

"There, that's sorted. Angie will sort out a date in time for the funeral then everybody can go – no problem! Just give us a date and time."

Angie said, "There were two things you wanted to ask about?"

"Oh yes. Do you want to stay for this bit?" he asked me, glancing at Angie. "It's about money."

"That's okay, anything you can say to me and all that," said Angie.

I was pleased, not only at this confirmation of our friendship but because I'm always fascinated by any discussion of the filthy stuff.

"It's about the Will: my dad left everything to me and you – his only child and his wife – with a bit for Hugo but, if you would accept it, I'd like to give you the lot. My practice is taking off, Allan's just made Senior Partner, we're fine, more than fine and I know about the flyers and you looking for work and all that and I know the mortgage on this place, obviously, and … I know I hurt you and—"

"You can't buy me back those years!" said Angie, looking furious. "I don't want *anything* from you – least of all your money! Waltzing in here, throwing your money about, am I expected to be grateful?"

I really wanted to interrupt at this point and mention other, more comfortable, avenues for revenge but she was in full-flood.

"Money can't buy you out of this, I don't want anything from you. I want you to leave. I'll come to the funeral but that's all and that's for your mum and dad – not you!"

Martin had got up to leave. "Well, just think about it, it can't be easy …" He looked to me for help but I could offer none. I followed after him towards the front door.

"She'll think about it, probably," I said, "but later."

He nodded thanks and headed out of the door.

The sun was shining. Our neighbours, Martin's ex-neighbours, were in their front garden spraying poison on the roses. They looked up as the door opened.

"Mr and Mrs Fizsimmon!" he said, rather flustered. "John and Edith! Good morning both!" as he began to head down the driveway.

I had not seen it done before but what he received from them both by way of reply was a cold silent stare. I saw Martin hesitate and look towards them as if wondering at the silence. Then I heard Mr Fitzsimmons mutter just loud enough to be sure to be heard, "Disgusting pervert."

"Good morning, Beth!" then said Mr Fitzsimmons, looking pointedly towards me, ignoring Martin's greeting.

Martin reached the end of the driveway. Edith called after him, quite loudly, "We're praying for your soul – for Angela's sake!"

Martin turned, just as he opened the car door, and looked at her a long moment. He had an expression in his eyes which I'd never seen there before. He looked like he had a mouthful to say to them but, looking to me, he said none of it but got in the car and drove off, not gracing them with an answer. I went back in the house without saying anything to either of them or waiting to hear any comments.

Praying for his soul? For Angela's sake? I

pondered as I walked back down the hallway. How did that work then? If someone has committed a mortal sin does the Almighty take up references? Was that normal practice before hurling a soul into purgatory?

"Young man, I see you have committed mortal sin; however, I see you have excellent references from some jolly decent types who often sell raffle tickets for my church roofs so I'll go easy on you."

It wasn't quite my view of God. And anyway, what was Martin supposed to have done exactly? Murdered anyone? Hurt anyone? Or just fallen in love with someone? Of course it was sex between men or between women that got everyone in a froth but All Kinds of Non-Reproductive Sex had used to be banned and punishable by all kinds of horrors by neurotic (and hypocritical) rulers. Masturbation had been considered a sin, along with any sexual act which could not, at least potentially, produce a child – *all* were considered 'perverse' and against Nature or God or the Hollywood Guidelines, whichever you worshipped. It was all about breeding – nothing about love or passion or desire. It made you feel like a prize pig developed for produce of fine litters. I wondered, as I reached the kitchen door, if I told Edith and John about some of the things I got up to with Simon and indeed Frank, which were not even slightly linked to reproduction, whether they would pray for my soul too?

And I knew they only had two children, presumably that meant they had only 'done it' on two occasions? I knew that sex is to love like chocolate is to food (very nice and exciting but better not try to live on it) but it is considered to be generally a part of adult, consenting relationships of all kinds. But maybe not for John and Edith's kind where it is only for making babies.

Angela was still in the kitchen looking unhappy and conflicted. I could hardly blame her. I told her about the encounter between Martin and the neighbours. She pulled a face, "Well they are very religious so you can't blame them. Always raising money for the church. Wish I hadn't told her now. He's done nothing to hurt them, they have no reason to say stuff like that. Knowing her, if he'd left me for another woman they'd have probably asked him and her round for coffee and wanted all the details!"

"Doesn't surprise me either," I said, emptying the dregs and pulling the kitchen curtains into place. "Edith's always been like that. I remember at a coffee morning – you were there – years ago, when Cheryl – do you remember Cheryl? – told us her daughter had come out as gay and Edith said how she *always* thought, when she heard of a man being gay, 'What a waste of a man!'"

"Oh yes, I remember."

"Well I thought about that afterwards. That must mean that Edith thinks that if a man doesn't sleep with her, or doesn't want to sleep with her, then his whole life is *wasted!* I was impressed. She must be one hell of a shag!"

I felt sad about Edith and John. As a certain kind of religious people I knew they took it upon themselves to make life as difficult as possible for anyone of a differing religion or none and had, for example, led a campaign against there being a mosque in town for people who worship the same god but in a different way *and* against the local school celebrating Duvali's Festival of Light – which seemed unreasonable. I had not agreed to sign the petition they had brought around and John had remonstrated with me until I had asked him what he thought about the Good Samaritan story. Samaritans, in Jesus' time, I'd seen in a documentary, having been the persecuted religious and cultural minority, I'd said to John that they probably weren't allowed their own place of worship or festivals either without some bigots somewhere getting up a petition. Relations between us had been a little on the strained side ever since. My own nodding-terms acquaintance with the bible I had developed in my school days had found a lot of references to Jesus going on about love and acceptance and inclusion but it seemed many of his present day followers believed he was only being sarcastic.

Chapter Five

Meetings

The rest of the day was spent finishing the wallpapering of Hugo and Mafwaney's room, then we had a really healthy salad kind of thing for tea followed by a chocolate trifle.

As always, I forgot it was recycling day until Angela reminded me with a note of urgency in her voice, which she seemed to reserve for Thursday evenings, in time for us to cram all we had by way of the recyclable into the various bags of the right colours in time for the collection. Angela had developed a strict routine of putting the bags out 'just in time' in order to rob the local magpies and crows of a free meal (and the cul-de-sac of a free scattering of leftovers and tins) so we always got to the kerbside a few minutes before 6 p.m. and at least a good twenty minutes before the recycling truck arrived with its banners of bits and pieces breaking loose from the wire cages in which the waste of a town was entrapped like a consignment of very untidy criminals being relocated. Our neighbours would do a similar thing; it was the nearest our street ever got to a street party these days, apart from the evenings of 'clap for the NHS' which had been a meagre and tenuous event in our close, most of its inhabitants being able to afford to go private and only dimly aware of what 'NHS' stood for except when they had contracted something complicated or needed an ambulance.

Since Hugo and family had left, Angela had declared her intention to use the recycling evenings as a chance to try and re-connect with her near-neighbours and to appear 'normal' after the icy, whirlwind gossip of Martin's leaving and the secretive times of her family's visit. During their stay we had got in the habit of hurtling to the kerbside, dropping the bags of kitchen and/or garden and/or un-recyclable waste to lie where they fell and racing back indoors, clutching the hand of whichever child had come along to be 'helpful' but whose skin-tone, if glimpsed, just might have led to riots. So, since they had gone, Angela, with me in supportive role, had taken to positively dawdling on the Thursday 'evenings out', lingering over the arrangement of the sacks of waste, rearranging them aesthetically and calling out friendly greetings to other inhabitants of the immediate environment whom we glimpsed among the clipped, manicured foliage and low walls.

One or two of our neighbours had replied to our flyers and we would nod surreptitiously at each other as sharers of a Great Secret. We wouldn't tell if they wouldn't about our clandestine business world of tax-free income and cut-price work. The dog theft served a purpose this particular week as it gave us all something in common apart from the weather and was a welcome change of topic for monosyllabic utterances of 'shocking' and 'terrible' and shakings of heads with sympathetic lookings towards the Harrisons' abode where the recycling sacks were already tidily in place.

Even the usually taciturn Mr John Fitzsimmons, Angela's most immediate neighbour with whom she shared a large hedge and who came out of his garden gate this evening with bags full of cuttings from it and heaved them onto the pavement side, seemed keen to talk today. We had heard his hedge cutter and shredder going most of the afternoon and smelled the burnt offerings of the barbecue so it was no surprise to see these fruits of his labours bursting at the seams of several garden-waste bags. Angela seemed determined to stick to her resolution, even after the morning's unpleasantness from the Fitzsimmons', and showed interest in what he had to say which, to give her credit, was more than I could achieve.

He greeted us cheerily; agreed it was 'terrible about

the dog' then shared some speculation about what had happened and why and 'strange characters hanging about the neighbourhood' and replied to Angela's query that no, neither he nor his wife would be going to the meeting tonight, they would have done but 'Edith was determined to finish the gardening' and he had to go to some social commitment or other which was all very fascinating but then, just as I was wondering if we were ever going to get back in the house and whether being friendly with neighbours really was worth all the pain, thankfully he heard his wife calling from the back garden and he started as if in alarm, shouted back that 'yes, dear, I've got them packed', showed us a plastic box he was holding which looked like it contained sandwiches.

"She does fuss over me!" he smiled and asked us the time as he had to rush to get a train at seven. We both glanced at our mobiles, told him the time, Angela commented he was cutting it a bit fine but he had already hurriedly turned to go, adding that the trip was to a workmate's retirement 'do' which was why he was 'dressed like this' – indicating the rather smart though a bit crumpled suit he was wearing. He almost ran to his car, got in, and drove off, waving to us as he passed. It felt all a bit comical and we couldn't help but smile at this deluge of information which just a little friendliness on our part had brought forth and which only seemed to prove that even normally unfriendly people did want chat and have interactions with each other, given the chance, however pointless.

Angela was smiling and said it was nice to feel we had at last developed some kind of friendship with our neighbours if only because we had all had a bit of a shock lately and that some of the ice between Angela and, at least, her immediate neighbours was apparently melting after the frostiness following Martin's departure and yesterday's rudeness. Now everyday chat was back on the cards. He had even nodded and smiled at me so maybe even I was being accepted too in this road where respectable people did not need, or have, either lodgers or divorces. I was reflecting that, maybe, all the reasons we don't talk with our neighbours are good ones but didn't say this out loud. Then the recycling truck arrived and its crew, some in high-vis jackets, busied themselves across the close to heave our various sacks of rubbish onto the back of the truck and drive it all away.

As social opportunities seemed to have waned for the time-being, we, having done our neighbourly duty, locked the doors and headed off to the meeting. We walked the distance down our cul-de-sac and along to the corner of the common where the Scout Hut sagged in resignation in the dusk.

Cars pulled up in the small car park. It was obviously An Event.

Inside, a table had been set up at one end and a plastic and wooden assortment of chairs set out in an optimistic number of regular rows facing it. I was relieved not to see any exercise mats. The front row was filled but the rows behind held a reducing number of occupants as they receded towards the door. I went to sit in the back row, envisaging a sharp exit, but Angela took my arm and pushed me towards the front rows where we sidled into two seats on the aisle. Nobody was talking. At the top table were five chairs, four were occupied by people in suits with glasses of water in front of them and a pad of paper. There was a jug in the middle of the table and a bottle of water. Nobody was going to be thirsty at this meeting.

A woman was moving around the hall, pulling the long curtains closed. The four people in suits watched us as we walked in and then watched others as they too entered the hall behind us. Eventually the sound of the door opening and closing and of people getting to their seats with scrapings of chair legs and coughings and greetings ceased and the hall became quiet. The rows in front of us were dotted with people, some of whom I thought I recognised from our neighbourhood and some strangers. Two young men came to sit just in front of us; one in a faded, red-checked, padded work-shirt with tattoos on his neck – I didn't recognise him but thought I had seen him somewhere before – and the other in a faded blue and white-striped jumper. I nudged Angela and nodded towards the tattoos peeking above the checked collar. Simon had tattoos all over his arms and elsewhere. I thought of them fondly then pondered the recent increased distance between us and the recurring cancellations. Affairs were not the same when they had dwindled into regular relationships with no impediment to togetherness; no need for surreptitious and secret times; no need for hours of excitement snatched from out of mundanity when the mundanity had itself got up and left and set up shop with its own hours of excitement.

The curtain-closer moved to the empty chair at the top table and opened her mouth to speak. I recognised her immediately and Angela nudged me so I knew she had too. It was our opposite neighbour, Mrs Harrison – Joan. Mr Harrison, Charles, was one of the seated, suited four. A late-comer or two came in at that moment and Mrs H closed her mouth as we all listened to Late Comers finding their chairs towards the front and the door creaking to a close, then Mrs H. opened her mouth again.

We were informed that she was pleased to see us all and that we were obviously as concerned as she was at 'recent events' and that the four people she was pleased to introduce to us were severally, the local councillor, the local MP, a victim of the 'recent crime wave', and an 'eyewitness'. It all sounded terribly exciting and I was glad I'd secreted a small phial of brandy in my handbag to help me contain the excitement – anticipation of which surreptitious support being the reason I'd persuaded Angela away from driving to the meeting. I took out the phial and offered it and we took sips during the following. The sweet smell hung on the dusty air but only a few heads turned.

The first speaker arose to the applause which followed his introduction. Mrs H led the applause then diminished into her chair so as not to hog the limelight or intrude on his moment of glory. It was Mr Harrison. He thanked us for this chance to tell of his trauma. Everyone's eyes were on him. The suited, top-table water-sippers all acquired drawn expressions of concern and empathy as he told his harrowing tale. I have to say I was moved.

There were catches in his voice and pauses while he took drinks of water and struggled to contain his emotion as he told his tale; of the beloved dog who was the main companion to himself and his wife in their older years, torn from them by callous hands in the dead of night and whisked away to no-one knew where, leaving them bereft and distraught, not knowing where their loyal friend might be languishing. It was not the money or the mere monetary value of their much pedigreed pooch that grieved them, but the loss of a friend, obviously stolen by unfeeling yobs who thought only of the thousands she was worth as a producer of future generations of champions. He had to stop at this point and hung his head to quell the tears and the Chair, his wife, helped him to his seat and led the applause as he sat and buried his face in a large pocket handkerchief which he pulled from his pocket. I doubt there was a dry eye in the place. I myself needed another swig of brandy.

It was the turn of our MP, not someone whom Angela or I had ever seen in the area before but he was someone we knew was well respected at the Golf Club and who could be seen at all the 'best parties' in the district (parties to which we were no longer invited, of course, following our newly acquired divorced/single/financially embarrassed and no-longer-quite-so-respectable status). The MP stood up and surveyed us all with a grave expression. He held an arm out towards the still emotionally overcome Mr H and his handkerchief.

"This," he intoned, "is what comes of being soft on the Criminal Element!" (He definitely said this with capital letters.)

Someone in the front row began to clap but stopped out of loneliness. Someone else was inspired to call out 'Here! Here!' pronouncing it 'Hyah-Hyah', but he hadn't finished.

"How long," he asked us, "are we expected to tolerate the presence of these ... people?"

A few hummed at this point. Angela was looking around her, wanting to identify the 'people' he was referring to. The rest of us knew whom he meant.

"Gypsies," he said, louder now, "or perhaps I should call them 'Travellers' as the Politically Correct Mafia would have it, have a lax attitude to right and wrong – as we all know."

There were more hums.

"Innocent people asleep in their beds having their beloved pets *ripped* from their arms!" His voice took on dramatic intonation and he raised his arms towards us by way of emphasis in case we weren't getting it.

"By dead of *night*!" His eyes bulged at the horror of this, as if a self-respecting burglar with any sense of decency would go about his or her business in broad daylight to give the law enforcement agencies a sporting chance.

He paused for dramatic effect. Then, "How long! How long are we going to tolerate this stain on our community!"

"Like animals!" someone called from the front rows, and, "They don't even live in houses!" someone else from across the aisle added more quietly. There was more sporadic clapping.

The MP waited then began again.

"We have here tonight an eye-witness who can tell us …' (at this point I felt myself flush red and I had the horrible notion I was going to be called on to tell of what I had seen from the upstairs window) '… all about it!"

But it wasn't me to whom the MP now gestured, it was a small woman at the end of the table who now stood up, smiling at the MP and the Chair who both led the applause of welcome as she stood.

We waited, bated breath, to hear of the horrors she had witnessed. She explained that she lived at the edge of the common, in one of a row of houses which lined one edge of the open space and so could see 'everything'.

You could have heard a pin drop. Images of human sacrifice, midnight debauchery, mayhem, murder, devil worship, and orgies at the very least swam through my mind and probably most of the other minds present. Angela turned to look at me in horror, mouth open.

"There's the empty school on the common …" she began. That was true, it had been empty for the past two years having been closed down and we waited to hear what horrendous rites had been performed in its benighted playground. "And they," she paused to take a breath to hit us with the full horror of her tale, "have been keeping a *horse* in it!"

For a moment I thought I'd misheard. Keeping a what, a hearse? A curse? No, a horse. There were mutterings of various levels of aghastness – someone stood up and took a photograph of her, blinding her with the flash. I noticed two people – one with the camera and one scribbling furiously – sitting near the front but there remained an air of expectancy as if more was wanted and the thirst for scandal and horror was even yet un-slaked. She seemed to sense this and added, "Sometimes *two* horses!" The Chair seemed to realise that there was no more horror to come and led another round of applause. The woman sat down, nodding happily that she had had the chance to tell of the trauma she had endured.

The MP stood up again. "That's what I mean! No respect for property! No regard for animals! No respect—"

But then, "How come the school's closed then?" called out someone from near the front.

It must have been one of the Latecomers. We all looked at the young woman who had called out. The Chair raised her hand as if to stop a bus.

"No heckling please – there will be time for questions later."

The MP acknowledged her with a nod and the Chair simpered at him. She glared briefly in the direction of the interruption and continued. The two young men sitting in front of us craned to see who it was who had called out and said something to each other I couldn't catch. The MP said more about the need to be vigilant and quite a bit more about his career in politics to date and the up-coming elections but I was distracted. I, and I expect everyone else, was now remembering why it was the school had been closed and who had led the campaign to close it and it certainly hadn't been the gypsies.

In the front row a couple of faces had appeared as they turned to look back at whoever it was who had asked the unwelcomed question. As they turned back to face the front again I noticed they had very short hair all over and were both wearing green bomber jackets with badges. I had seen people dressed and coiffured like that before, giving out leaflets in the town centre. I glanced at Angela to see if she had noticed but it was her turn with the phial of brandy and she was looking up at the rafters and at the photographs of ranks of uniformed youth on the walls around the hall next to the Union Jack.

The MP sat down and the next person to speak and entertain us was a policeman who told us they were doing everything to find the missing dog and return her to her family and urged us to do everything in our power to help the police and see that justice was done. There was quite a lot of stuff about how to make our homes secured and to look out for each other's safety and moves that were 'under review' to close off the common 'for the safety of our citizens.' I was bored by now and had run out of brandy. The policeman sat down.

The Chair stood and thanked us all for coming, invited us for a drink at the ... but someone coughed. The Chair looked towards the sound irritably. Two hands were held in the air. It was the latecomers again. The young woman was holding her hand in the air and seemed to have been doing so for quite a while as she was supporting the raised arm with the other as if she was getting tired. She wore a patient expression. The young man who was sat next to her was also holding his hand up and also looking determined. The Chair seemed unsure what to do as we all looked at her expectantly.

"I still have some questions," called out the young woman. It was she who had asked about the closed school.

The Chair looked uncertain and looked to the MP for support but he nodded. The guys in green turned around to look as well-. I could see now there were three of them – all in green jackets with badges and all had shaved or cropped heads.

"Yes we'll allow some questions," said the Chair, "if there's time."

"I live near the common too," said the young

woman, "my kids used to go to that school – why did you campaign to close it? My kids have to bus it miles away now. And the Gypsies cause no trouble, my kids play with their kids no problem and they helped sort our old car out as well. So what they keep a horse there? The crime is that it's empty and it's not the Gypsies who closed it, is it—?"

The Chair interrupted, "What is your question?" She sounded cross. One of the green jackets had partly stood up and was giving the questioner what could only be called a 'hard stare'.

"The question is," the young woman resumed, speaking more slowly, "how come you lot are holding this meeting? I never see you around here in between elections. Is there any evidence any of the Travellers have stolen that dog? Or done anything wrong at all? This is just—"

"That's quite enough," said the Chair. "Any further questions?"

"You lot are just saying bad things about people you don't even know! This is just scapegoating – it's just prejudice and racism!" the young woman continued, louder.

The Chair stood up, she looked furious as she said, "This is NOT racism – everybody knows what Travellers are like!"

There was not a hint that she was at all aware of

the irony of what she had just said.

Then, suddenly, another voice, very close to me, stammered loudly, "It is … it *is* racism! This is what pe-people do to my grandkids … people like my grandkids. My grandkids … just because … my grandkids are … This isn't fair, there's no *evidence*. So *what* about the horse? It *is* prejudice!" The Chair hit her hand down on her table and stood up, her eyes angry, mouth petulant. She took a breath to make her voice return to its dinner-party smoothness and she smiled through the glare that was threatening to show itself.

"PLEASE don't shout out – don't heckle," she said that word as if it was something dirty, "if you raise your hands I will take questions one at a time in the proper manner." She looked pointedly in our direction and I realised it had indeed been Angie who had called out about her grandchildren and I looked at her in amazement as she raised her hand. Her hand was trembling, she was looking wide-eyed at the chairwoman like a rabbit in headlights and she had gone beetroot red but she raised it. Faces were turned towards us. The reporter was looking over towards us then made some more notes.

Mrs H nodded curtly at Angela who stood up in a sort of hunched way, I noticed she was gripping the back of the chair in front, making the young man lean forward and turn around to look up at her, and that her legs were shaking while she said in a trembling voice, "I know some children who get accused of stealing just because they are … they have dark skin but they never steal anything. And *they* get called names. They get bullied … and they're really good kids. And … this is the same. It isn't right. You don't *know* who stole the dog! And … and … the gypsies have always been here – every year."

Her voice was a bit high pitched but it was clear enough. She seemed to run out of steam and turned to sit down. The reporter had turned in his chair and looked at Angie expectantly but she was shocked at her own outburst and became silent, blushing furiously. I saw a few of our neighbours looking at her as if they had never seen her before and exchanging telling glances with each other with raised eyebrows.

But somehow the atmosphere in the room had changed, and another hand was raised. This one was brown and the man raising it wore a turban. The Chair looked around for another hand but there weren't any so she acknowledged him and he stood up slowly. He was grey-bearded and quite portly. People turned to hear him. He looked around him as he spoke.

"You all know me," he began, he had a slight accent and spoke delicately. "You know my family, you know my work, I've visited many of your houses to fix your plumbings and washing machines. We play cricket together on the common in the summer. You all speak to me. Our children became friends together as they grew up. They went to that school too." He paused. "But it wasn't always like that, was it?" he continued quietly. There was a quiet in the room. Some people were looking down at the floor.

The Chair looked as if she wanted to speak but then closed her mouth. The MP's face was a closed book.

The man in the turban continued quietly: "What is being said about the people on the common – the Travellers or Gypsies – the same was said about me when we came to this country, wasn't it? We were thieves and murderers and had diseases and the rest of it. And worse. My children were called names at school, my wife was spat at in the street, had a headscarf pulled off, we had dog mess pushed through our door, I was called names every day at work ... and the Government," he looked at the top table and the MP, "told everyone that *we* were causing all the job losses and closures. Is there any evidence it was the Gypsy family who took the dog? I know them– they fixed my car too. Gypsies have been coming here for years, centuries before the town was even built, before there even was a 'common'. They don't seem to want to steal anything. Why have you come here to stir up hatred? You don't usually come here or pay any attention to people's concerns until you want our votes. I have had enough of hate for one lifetime and the lady's right." He nodded towards Angela, "This is just racism and it's as ugly as ever.

That is all I want to say – thank you."

He sat down.

Angela wasn't the first to start clapping but hers was the loudest. I looked at her in amazement as others joined in but then I remembered what Mafwaney had said and remembered the grandchildren who called me 'auntie' and had to keep their hands in their pockets to avoid being accused of stealing and who got called names at school and I began to clap too.

Then someone at the front sprang up, someone in a green jacket with badges. "We all know it was them. They live in caravans, not like real people, we all know it I don't care what you say.." This one was blustering and red in the face with anger. His neighbour put a hand on his arm to coax him to sit back down and he did, still red faced.

People had got up to leave and began heading for the door. Mrs Harrison, as Chair, stood up and declared that the meeting was over, her voice a bit high pitched and desperate sounding, and she expressed the wish that everyone would join them for drinks at the local pub not far from the Scouts' Hall but not many seemed to hear her though she said it twice. A little group had gathered around the guy with the turban and there seemed to be much handshaking and shoulder patting going on there. He was smiling in an embarrassed way. The reporter turned to look at Angie then came over with his notebook, the photographer followed.

"I'm from the *Gazette*," he said. "About what you said, would you say a bit more about your grandchildren, about what you think of the Gypsies on the common?"

Angie shook her head, "I don't want my grandchildren to be in the paper, they get picked on same as the Gypsies do – that's all."

"Can I have your name? Can you give me a quote? It was very brave of you speaking out like that. Are you local?" But we moved away and left him with his notebook. The photographer came up with his camera but we turned away. Some of our near- neighbours were looking at us in an unfriendly way. Angela pushed up against me and I took her arm. A very quiet elderly couple who lived at the top of the road, and whom we saw walking past our gate very occasionally, came towards us but we headed for the door, not wanting to give them time to speak. It looked like Angela's hopes of building friendships in the neighbourhood might have come to an untimely end.

When we got to the door the two Latecomers, the young woman and her bespectacled male companion, were proffering a petition on a clipboard calling for 'no to racism' and we stopped to sign it – at least

Angela did, I hovered uncertainly. I don't usually get involved and this was more 'involved' than was healthy, I was sure.

As we stood, Angela with her head down with pen in hand, writing on the petition, suddenly the booted green-jacketed ones arrived from behind us, shouldered me out of the way, grabbed the petition she was holding, threw it to the floor, shoving her backwards, then one thrust his face, contorted with rage, down into the young woman's face calling her a 'gyppo-lover' and other names. Another recognised Angela and thrust his sneering face into hers. "So, your grandchildren are little——?" but he never got to the next word because a brown hand had grabbed the back of his shirt collar, a white hand had seized his shirt front and he was pulled and pushed by two or three people roughly away from us until he fell to the floor. He was a big man and his two companions were on the large side too and looked used to violence but they were taken by surprise and outnumbered.

"That's where you belong! You stay there!" said one of his assailants, whom I realised was the young bespectacled one and who was red with anger. Among the group also were the guy in the turban, the guy in the faded striped jersey, the reporter, and the one in the red checked shirt with tattoos. The photographer took a picture of the man on the floor as he struggled to his feet, breathing heavily. The three green-jacketed ones glared at us all as we stood facing them. I was rather nearer the front than felt entirely comfortable but the young woman with the clipboard came to stand next to me and I pulled myself together, we outnumbered them nearly ten-to-one after all.

Then suddenly the two young men who had been sitting in front of us in the meeting stepped forward from the crowd towards the three skinheads and stood glaring right back at them, arms folded. At least that is what seemed to be happening from what we could see of the back of their heads. The skinheads' faces looked unsure and as if they thought they were about to be attacked but the two young men stood for a few moments in front of us, quite still, arms folded, until they had the skinheads' full attention. Then the one in the red shirt leaned forward and, quite deliberately, spat on the floor towards the skinheads' feet. Then, unhurriedly, the two stepped towards the door without breaking eye contact with the three in green, the rest of us sidled out of the way to let them through, and then, with the same fixed expression, the two stood in the doorway for a moment, staring at the skinheads, unmoving. Then the two left the hall and we heard them head out into the night.

It was like an unspoken invitation, a challenge; the three green-jacketed ones looked at each other and seemed to have a silent consultation – they seemed unsure what to do. Then the biggest of them swore, "F-ng pykies!" and as one, they ran towards the door and out into the gathering night, their faces set and hard. We watched them go and could just hear many running footsteps fading away outside.

As soon as they had gone we all felt the whole room become more relaxed. The reporter picked up the petition, straightened it on its board, and returned it to its owner. The two with the petition had also been harassed and pushed but had been protected by the small crowd and were quite alright apart from tousled clothes and displaced glasses. The retrieved petition was offered again and the signing continued with most people signing it. As we left the hall we could see the Chair and the speakers, who didn't seem to have noticed events by the door, putting on their coats. Only a very few others seemed to have accepted the invitation to go for a drink and were hovering near them.

"They might be waiting outside," someone had suggested and we all agreed to leave the hall together and see each other to cars. It was sorted out among everyone there with quick discussions – who had cars and who needed a lift – no-one was to be left to walk or be alone in the night. We had all noticed the badges on the green jackets, the swastikas and the miniature union jacks.

"We're walking," said Angela, to the crowd in general. She was a little slurred and I nodded a little vaguely at her clear definition of the situation.

"You can come with us?" offered the young woman and her male companions with the petitions and we accepted. There was no sign of the three men in green jackets with large boots, or the two others, but the small light above the hall door only penetrated the dark night a few yards in each direction, beyond which was all darkness and empty common.

"That was really good what you said," the young woman was addressing Angela, who nodded and blushed. "Better not walk back, you know what they're like. Actually we're going to go back via the camp thought. We'd better warn the Travellers that they're about, just in case. You can come too if you want?"

Chapter Six

Another Visit

We left the hall and the little crowd around us dispersed towards various cars and a few bicycles, lights switched on but the night seemed very dark with the thought of booted nazis lurking behind bushes looking for people who disagreed with them. The reporter and the photographer caught up with us and offered a lift with them but we had already accepted our first offer.

"Can I at least have your name?" the reporter asked Angela, "I'm Geraint."

"Angela," said Angela, and Geraint, middle-aged and balding, watched her walk away with a strange look in his eyes – or it might have been the brandy affecting my perception.

We followed the two young people and I found myself outside the kind of car into which I would not normally consider climbing but the front door was open and the front seat propped forward for my convenience. Angela had already crawled, and I use the word most advisedly, into its darker environs and the young woman was holding the door open for me, her companion already ensconced in the passenger seat, so I got in.

We headed up to the main part of the common, our benefactors discussing the finer points of the meeting and its possible political implications as we headed into the night, turning off the main road onto a kind of track.

"He knew they'd be there if he had a meeting like that!" the young woman was saying. "He won't throw a firebomb himself but he's quite happy that others might! But at least the meeting didn't go how they wanted it to, which is good. They might not have the confidence now to do anything more. We'd better go and warn them though that they're about in case they do try anything."

Her companion nodded, asked us if we knew the MP in question, but otherwise was content to look out for potholes in the road ahead.

I wasn't too sure what or who she meant and was lost among the many pronouns but nodded. I wanted to tell her I was glad she had spoken up as it had made it easier for others to speak but I couldn't find the right phrase.

We left the distant street lights behind us and turned off the main road and along a track which ran along next to the dried up stream that had used to run across the common until recent years. After a while we could see the silhouettes of trees against the dark sky and the squarer, solid, white shapes of caravans in the light of a fire, burning orange and yellow with silhouettes of people moving across it. As we came closer we could see the brightly lit faces of others tending the fire or sitting on the other side of it. Some children and a dog were running about and there were shapes of cars on the edge of the wavering circle of light. Something seemed to be cooking in a pot hung from a tripod to one side of the main flames and a figure attended to its contents. The derelict school building with its boarded-up windows and air of neglect was just visible beyond the circle of flickering firelight. I couldn't see if any scandalous horses were lurking within it, terrorising the neighbourhood.

Our driver parked the car next to one of the caravans, got out, and pulled the seat forward to facilitate our getting out of the back. We hesitated. She nodded encouragingly. Her companion was already out and was exchanging greetings with some of the people around the fire.

"It's okay," she said, seeing our expressions. "These aren't the people you need to be afraid of."

I got out, Angela followed, and we walked over towards the fire. Some younger ones were heaved out of a couple of folding chairs and we were invited to sit near the warmth. Our companions were reporting about the meeting to a couple who were older than the others – about the same age as Angela and me – whom they seemed to know.

The older man then said, "My eldest, Billy, and his cousin Liam were both there, they went along to see what happened. We knew it would be about us, it's always about us," he said. "They'll tell us more when they get back. Thank you for what you did."

He turned towards us, "I hear you spoke up for us?" he said to Angela and me. Our young companions introduced him as 'Da'. I nodded and saw Angela doing similar out of the corner of my eye. Da and others looked at us, expectantly, but it became obvious we were not the talkative type. Mugs of a hot substance were pressed upon us by an older woman who wore a lot of shawls and a long skirt. There was some talk in a language I did not recognise. Our companions were also given cupfuls of something and offered chairs.

"It was good of you to come and warn us," said Da, which triggered another round of smiles in our direction. "We can cope with shouts of filthy language, lies in the press and even dog mess thrown at us, but that type can throw firebombs in the night."

There were unhappy nods and murmurs of assent. We all looked at the small children who were still running about with their dog in the edge of the light, laughing.

"A lot of people signed the petition though," said the young woman, "they're not all like that."

Da said, with a smile, "That's great, young miss, but we can't rely on bits of paper to keep us safe."

"We'll keep watch tonight," said a young man.

"You will not," said Da. "You have work tomorrow and your bairns need your wage. Billy and Liam can do it when they get back. Liam's place has closed so he's laid off and Billy's only on casual."

This was said with quiet authority and was accepted without a murmur. Another log was thrown on the fire. I nursed the hot cup in my hands. Ideas about wicked deeds by Gypsies flittered across my mind from lost recesses of childhood where they haunted stories as baddies and murderers. One of the young women was eyeing me and whispered something to her friend as they both looked at me with interest. I wondered if my clothes impressed them.

"Your first time at a Gypsy camp?" the older woman said, addressing Angela and me.

I began to nod again but managed a 'yes' this time. She indicated the cup I was holding.

"It is only tea you know," she raised her own mug and took a sip as if to reassure me, "we don't poison visitors before midnight, as a general rule."

"Not on a Thursday night anyway," added someone else.

This brought some smiles and laughter around the warm circle. Embarrassed, I took a sip of the hot liquid – it was tea, and quite delicious with sugar. There were a lot of amused smiles in my direction and the ice felt like it had melted a little, but before I could say anything conversational, sounds coming from behind alerted us to more people arriving. Two young men entered the lit circle: I recognised the one in the red checked shirt with tattoos on his neck and the one in the blue-and-white jersey. People stopped talking as the two entered the circle to sit on logs laid near the fire. They had a brief conversation with Da in their own language and he nodded and seemed satisfied and the group gave a low cheer. The two then saw us and nodded in our direction and said something about us to the others and we had more warm looks. They also greeted the young couple who had brought us, who had obviously been here before and seemed to know everyone.

Da then said in English, "Well, two of them won't be bothering us tonight – the other one ran away – dirty cowards they are but we don't know how many there might be in the town, so you take watch tonight.

Well done both." He nodded at the two young men then looked at us. He must have seen the look on my face as he smiled again, eyes sparkling with humour, "Only a broken nose and a few bruises, maybe some lost teeth, nothing worse," he said. "They'll recover. That sort only like fighting people when we're sleeping or they're happy abusing our kids, they don't like a couple of talented boxers taking them on. A 'pre-emptive strike' I think they'd call it!."

There was some pride in his voice as he indicated the two young men as he spoke. The two acknowledged the second low cheer that greeted this and raised their arms and clenched fists. Then the old man's tone changed quite suddenly as he continued in sudden anger, "There's blood on your hands still!" he cried. "And no doubt those scum will go straight to the police and the cops will be here looking for you for assault and you have enough evidence on your hands to shop you. You young eejits! You're not sleeping here tonight in case the police come for you. But we need you here in case the boot-boys attack, so fetch what you need and disappear for the night but stay in easy reach. And get that stuff washed off!"

He was more stressed than angry with trying to balance the needs of his family against the forces against them. His son and nephew both towered over him but looked cowed and went to fetch 'what they needed'. I noticed some of their knuckles and forearms were indeed bloody. So did the older woman and she said something to them, apparently directing them to go and wash and put on bandages as they went away and we heard splashing water over by some cans and containers.

Da looked over towards us and said quietly, "The police are not too interested when we get attacked or when our homes get burned and they're happy to move us on and take our homes but they get *really* excited if they can catch us defending ourselves."

Our young companions, our 'ride', got up to go. They told Da they could offer to be witnesses if there were any charges brought as Billy and Liam had *not* started the fighting. Da thanked them and they swapped phone numbers. They looked to us to signal it was time to go. We finished our tea and handed over the mugs to various hands.

Da stood up, "Thank you for your help all – we'll take it from here."

"Any more news about Jimmy?" someone asked. People shook their heads.

"Tried to see him today but 'No Visitors Allowed'," said the young woman who had taken an interest in my outfit.

There was a general murmur of anger at this further evidence of cruelty and made-up rules that only apply to some people, not most. The older woman stared into the fire. I could see the grim lines of her face in the firelight. I noticed for the first time that her eyes had dark rings and all the signs of the sleepless nights and anxiety when one of our children is in danger. One of the younger women put an arm across her shoulders and looked at her in concern. There was a short silence.

I remembered with a shock why we were there and why all this had happened, the stolen dog, and that I might know something about that which no-one else did. But I didn't know what to say that wouldn't sound as stupid as the first time I'd said it. We were already stood up and on our way back towards the little car. Conversation in their own language had already resumed.

The two young men with bloodied and bandaged fists collected what looked like a tarpaulin and some smaller bags and headed off into the night. The older woman handed them some wrapped packets as they left.

"They'll go and camp out on the common away from the others and out of sight in case the police come here looking for them," said our driver. "At least they made it less likely the nazis will turn up tonight. Nazis are cowards – like all bullies."

We got dropped off at the end of our road, and the little car headed off into the night. The young woman

— she had said her name and that of her companion but I'd already forgotten them — gave us some blank copies of the petition and suggested we get more names to show the council that local people were not *all* against the Travellers being there and we walked home. It was pitch dark and the street light was on. There was no wind at all and no moon showed.

I had an idea. "Look, the Harrisons are probably still at the pub for a while, you go upstairs and look out and tell me what you see. I'll do what I saw that woman doing that night, it's a still night. Just see what you can hear and see." Angela looked at me as if I was mad but then cottoned on and went in the house. I waited until I saw the upstairs window open and I could see Angela's pale face in the orange light of the streetlamp. The brandy was helping against the cold.

I then walked over to the top of the Harrison's drive, I waved to Angela and she waved back. There was no-one about. I mimed getting out of a car and then walked quickly down the drive, my shoes crunching on the gravel. I moved around the car that was parked there. I realised they must have driven their other one to the meeting so I made a mental note that they may return at any moment and listened for the noise of a car approaching.

I got to the front of the house, ducking down as I had seen the woman do. In the streetlamp's light I could not see anything but a letterbox at the bottom of the door, a milk delivery rack, and one of those brass things to wipe your shoes on, then I turned and headed around the side of the house. It was pitch black here, the shadow of the house blocking out the streetlight. I felt my way between the house wall and the garden fence until I was stopped by an obstacle across my path which I explored with my fingers. It was a metal garden gate which I could barely see in the gloom and which would keep the back garden secure and dog-proof. My hands found the shape of a padlock. Turning to feel my way back, my fingers lost contact with the brick wall's roughness and I found a recess and then a window frame.

I could only sense it by touch, the cold smoothness of glass, but its angle was wrong, it was sloped vey slightly. I felt upwards and found the warmer roughness of the frame and the edge along its top where the frame stuck out, leaving a gap where it was jammed shut but the frame wasn't flush. Using my phone torch I could see a slight gap where it was jammed slightly out of its frame. There was a tiny gap at one corner, not big enough for a hand or finger – hardly big enough for even a draught – and not easily visible.

I headed back, walked up the drive, imagining a dog beside me, and mimed getting in the car and closing the door. I checked the road for intruders then returned home.

"Well?" Angela looked at me blankly.

"That was a re-enactment," I said. She wasn't the only one who watched police programmes. "What did you see?"

She shrugged. "I saw you go down the drive. I could hear your steps on the gravel, you went to the door then around the side of the house——"

"You could hear my steps, so you would have heard breaking glass? Did you see me bend down at the door?"

"Yes, what were you doing?"

"Not sure. So that was all clear. Could I have got to the front door without you seeing me?"

"No, the streetlight lit up the whole house-front, the car and the door. I could see you quite clearly moving across. I couldn't see your feet but that was all and if you'd broken the front door glass I'd definitely have heard it! I could even hear your footsteps. What's down the side?"

"There's a window."

"Oh. Is that all? Fancy a coffee?"

We went and had a nightcap and I helped Angela with her homework which consisted of watching a film called *Rear Window* and noting film angles and lighting. It was very entertaining despite a ridiculously unrealistic plot.

"Oh, by the way, I found this by the door when I came in," said Angela.

She held up a small blue pot with a tiny bunch of flowers in it in some water. It was very pretty. There was no note or clue who had put it there.

I went to lock the door and noticed the Harrison's second car pulling into the drive on their return home.

Chapter Seven

In the Details

In the kitchen the next day, over lunch, Angela was nibbling a biccie and looking at the paper.

"Have you seen this?" she said.

A report about the meeting was all over the front page of the local *Gazette*, or at least a report about an event which neither Angela nor myself much recognised but which was entitled, 'Brawl at Public Meeting over Gypsy Encampment' with a smaller headline: 'Dog Theft, Arrest Made' just next to it.

There was a picture of the MP, wearing an expression of outraged decency, quoted as saying 'There was no trouble like this in the area before the Travellers arrived' (which was untrue as 'trouble like this' happened most weekends in the drinking area of town, especially on Saturdays), and a rather blurred picture inset of an indistinct figure in green apparently fallen on the floor. Mrs Henderson was also quoted as saying how heartrending it was 'not knowing what had become of their beloved dog'. There followed an account of the 'terrorised community living in fear of burglary and theft of their pets', which made me think that maybe I ought to be living in fear, plus another reference to the police having made an arrest the previous day at the 'nearby Gypsy encampment on the common which has been at the centre of the controversy which prompted the meeting to try and address the concerns of local people but which was broken up by violent scuffles'. The report said in the next sentence that some supporters of the Travellers had 'invaded' the meeting. The way it was written gave the strong implication that it was they who had been the cause of the 'scuffles'. No mention was made of any nazis or of people being pushed or yelled at.

The MP was quoted as being appalled at such behaviour and determined to not be 'intimidated by such thuggery.'

"The Travellers didn't cause any trouble! It was those idiots in green jackets!" exclaimed Angela to nobody in particular. "And that nasty man in his suit was just stirring them up!"

Opposite the photograph of the heroic-looking MP was another copy of the inset photograph of the young man who'd been arrested. He was looking wide-eyed at the camera, was that an aggressive stare?

Or was it fear? He had a thin, square face and sported the kind of facial hair which very young men often sport when they do not wish to appear quite so young. He was not wearing a suit and his hair was short and dreadlocked. The caption read, 'Suspect in pet dog theft arrested at Traveller site: police investigating.' I looked at the photograph.

"That's not the face I saw. That's not the woman I saw take the dog and it's not the face of the guy driving the car either. I saw them both as the car turned around. She had a pointed sort of chin and lots of hair and he had glasses, sideburns, and red hair!"

"You sure?"

"Positive. It might have been blonde. But neither of the people I saw looked anything like that young lad!"

"What do we do?"

"I don't know. Do we really want to get involved?"

"I think we are involved."

"But we tried to talk to the police and they didn't listen. They obviously thought I was just a silly old woman! And the Harrisons didn't seem to want to know either!"

"Try again?"

"So they won't listen again? And what about this stupid report? It wasn't even like that!"

There didn't seem to be anything we could do.

Except …

"I know," said Angela, "let's go and talk to them."

"Who?"

"The Travellers. Tell them what you saw."

"What good would that do? What could they do?"

"I don't know, I just think … I don't know but we should tell people."

"But we don't really know them," I said weakly.

"Well, we're not getting very far with people we *do* know so let's branch out a little!"

"Will it be safe, on our own?"

"Well, not if you believe what it says in the paper. I want a word with that reporter for a start about that twaddle he's written. We met the Travellers last night and they were alright, weren't they?"

"Yes," I said hesitantly.

"*And* they gave us some tea!"

That seemed to be the deciding factor. I wanted to say something cautionary about the forces of evil deceiving us with gifts of false friendship but she didn't seem to be in the mood.

She was folding the newspaper into her bag and fetching her coat and car keys. It seemed a decision had been made. I sometimes felt I didn't know Angela lately – this was a new and decisive Angela. Something had 'got in amongst her' as my dad would have said. She headed out to the car and I meekly followed.

Arriving on the common in daylight, we could see the small group of trailers parked over by some of the few trees which graced the common with their sparse, early Spring foliage over the well-cropped grass which was usually only home to various cows, ponies, summertime wildfires and rumours of wildlife. Today, three piebald or skewbald shire-type horses were tethered and grazing near the trailers. A young child was leading one over to where some buckets of water awaited. The child came up to about one of the horses' knees but the horse seemed to have every confidence in its young charge. One of the caravans was of the old-fashioned kind with wooden wheels, arched roof, and tiny windows, but the others were of a more modern, stark-white and metal variety. A wheeled cart rested forward on its runners with what looked like a washing machine standing bizarrely next to it. We parked up on the edge of the road and sat looking at the site.

"What are we doing here?" seemed to be the big, unspoken question as we sat in the car surveying the scene. It all looked very alien.

There was a pause. Neither Bravado nor

Decisiveness had accompanied us, apparently.

"I think we're trying to do the right thing," I suggested as an answer to the gathering silence.

"Maybe you're right and we shouldn't interfere," said Angela, her hand on the ignition key.

I too wanted to drive away.

"Come on, they were fine with us last night," I said. "We can at least try and put something right. Probably won't get anywhere but we can at least try."

We got out of the car. It was a mild, cloudy afternoon. We walked towards the camp.

There were two cars parked near the caravans which we had seen silhouetted last night but as we neared we could now see that one was up on bricks and the other had its bonnet open. These were the centre of attention of three young men leaning into the engines, plus a younger teenager standing in attendance, holding an oil can and a metal tool of some kind.

Clothes flapped on lines hung between the trailers and the trees. Some bin bags, tied at the top, sat outside the ring of trailers in a heap. Last night's fire was a blackened ring and the pots were upturned near the containers of water, drying in the sun. Three small children and a dog were playing some sort of tag farther out on the common. The dog was wearing a t-shirt and shorts, the shorts were on backwards which allowed its tail to stick out of the fly-hole. It bounded around the children, its tail wagging slowly, its tongue hanging out in the daft grin of its kind.

The men near the cars glanced up as we approached but then turned back to the engines they were working on. The older woman from last night appeared from around one of the trailers carrying a basket of wet clothes. There were bags and baskets of what looked like laundry lying on the ground. She headed towards us, frowning against the bright sunlight. She was looking past us, over our shoulders, but then recognised us and held out a hand for us to shake.

"I'm Pearl," she said, simply, "I was looking to see what trouble you had brought with you but then I recognised you from last night. You are welcome."

The men had glanced over at us but greeting visitors seemed to be her remit. Pearl looked at us enquiringly.

I said, "Did you have any more trouble last night?"

Pearl shook her head, watching us closely. "Not the kind you mean anyway. We kept watch, no skinheads showed up. Police showed up looking for Billy and Liam though. Those nazis *did* go to them and complained just like we thought they would. Billy and Liam are both wanted for assault. But they didn't look far for them, they'd only gone onto the common within earshot to sleep and keep safe and keep watch. We told the police they had left, which was true in a way. The police poked about the place, said they were looking for 'stolen goods', cheeky sods. I asked them for a warrant, they didn't have one of course for all the difference that makes but at least they went away to get one. The two boys came back this morning. They got a change of clothes and a bite to eat. They were tired after sleeping out but they're young! Billy is Jimmy's older brother – Jimmy's my youngest – he's been arrested for supposedly stealing some dog or other. Liam's their cousin." She nodded over to where the two young men we recognised and one other were bent over the old cars.

Then I said, "I think I know something that might be important. Might be helpful."

She studied my face and I knew what it felt like to be fully looked at. She put down the bowl of wet washing and finished wringing out one of the shirts before straightening up with a grimace, drying her hands on her apron, and turned to give us her full attention. I thought of my washer-drier. It was obvious all the laundry here was done by hand and dried in the sun. She saw me looking and commented, "I take in washing for people who want things hand-washed – silk and the like, nice things that can't cope with hot water," she nodded towards the clothes lines where some elegant and fragile finery hung in the sunshine.

I'd lost my train of thought.

"Go on," she said.

"It's about the dog," I said, remembering.

"We're not dog thieves," she said. "Rex is the only dog we've got or need. Jimmy, his brother and cousins, they're mechanics, they're boxers, they're gardeners, they're fruit-pickers, they're road-workers, so is my husband, Da. We're not thieves. Jimmy was the only one home that night, so he was the only one without an alibi. They didn't believe me of course, he was in his trailer doing work for his college course. That'll all be off now as well if he gets done for this—"

"But he won't, will he," said Angie, "if he's innocent?"

She looked at us and said, "You believe that if it helps you, my dear," and I felt that she was, after all, a lot older than I was and knew things I didn't.

"Yes but they reckon it's probably a gang."

"Yeh, head of a huge operation, I am!" she said. We looked with her at the dusty site and the broken cars and the washing flapping in the wind. Her own clothes and those of the children were clean but patched and faded.

I gave a brief outline of what I had seen. She paid more attention than had my previous audience.

"You think you can help Jimmy?"

"We can try," I said. "We can talk to them again."

A twitch of an eyebrow told us what she thought the outcome of that effort would probably be.

"They've got their nick, he's got no alibi they need to listen to. Why would they look any further?"

We were silent for a moment.

"What car was it they had? What sort?" she asked.

I shook my head, cars are not one of my strong points. I told what I could remember.

"Beige with an orange roof? Bit unusual," she surmised and called to two of the men, "Billy! Liam!"

The men working on the cars hadn't taken much notice of us until then but they came when called, wiping their hands on a couple of oily rags they had tucked in their belts. I recognised the two young men from the meeting. Billy was the one who had been wearing the checked shirt and the other, Liam, had been wearing the blue-and-white jumper. Both had plasters on their knuckles in amongst the oil and Liam had a dark bruise on his cheekbone. I remembered they were both wanted by the police for allegedly attacking the three skinheads.

The children had resumed their game. Apparently we were no cause for alarm.

The two eyed us with curiosity. They too looked wary of what trouble we might bring. Pearl gave them an update as to why we were there.

"An old car, beige, orange roof, the lady says," she said. "Doesn't know what make."

Like his mother, Billy's eyes were bright blue and not even slightly naive as he looked at us.

He didn't look pleased at our news. I was to remember that later.

He said, "Unusual colour scheme for a car. Two or four door was it?"

I thought for a second, "Four. She put the dog in the back seat. It looked really new, shiny, but it was an old car – small."

I was embarrassed again, remembering how stupid this had sounded to the policeman and hearing how stupid it sounded now.

Billy shook his head, "Don't know any cars that colour – beige and orange? Must be a custom job."

Liam snorted. "Don't be daft! Who'd pay to have their car sprayed beige? The Really Boring Liberation Front?"

This broke the ice as we all smiled at this.

"Old, you say?"

"Yes but it looked brand new … not old like an old battered car, not rusty or anything …" my voice trailed away.

"Do you mean it was 'vintage'?" said Billy.

That was the word I'd been hunting for.

"Yes, vintage! It was vintage!"

Billy frowned and considered. "Beige? Anything you noticed about the shape? The tyres?"

I pondered. The car had rung a bell when I'd seen it, it had seemed familiar somehow but I couldn't say why.

"Have you seen it in the area?"

"No," I was sure about that, although … I knew I had seen it somewhere before.

"Could have driven in from anywhere," his mother pointed out.

"To pinch a dog? An outfit would have a van, wouldn't they, to pinch lots of dogs, not just a little car. Why just one? Have there been other dogs taken in the area do you know?" he asked us.

"No," said Angela, "the police said so." She blushed again as all eyes turned to her.

"They wouldn't drive miles for one dog, would they?" Liam speculated. "How did they get in the house? And how would they know it was there? Was it in the garden?"

We explained about the broken pane in the front door. About the open-plan front garden where no dog could roam safely as it was open to the road. About how the padlocked back garden was not visible from the road. About how we rarely saw any dogs from that house as they were kept in the back garden or the house and they usually only went out in cars to shows or we'd glimpse them sometimes driving off with new owners when the puppies were being sold off each year.

"They breed them then?" asked Liam who looked quite a few years younger than his cousin.

We nodded. "It's a valuable dog that has been taken."

Billy called to the other man working on the cars and he came over. He walked with a heavy limp, swinging his leg on each stride as if his leg joints no longer worked properly. I couldn't help staring in curiosity as he limped over.

"Accident at work," muttered Liam quietly, leaning towards me. "Some things he can't do, but some things he can do. We focus on those he can and we don't stare either!"

Embarrassed, I muttered an apology and stopped being so rude.

He was introduced as Matthew whose son was close in age to Jimmy and was his 'chavvy', whatever that meant. Also, as I couldn't help noticing, we were in a circle of younger men with oily tee-shirts and patched jeans, which was quite unusual, in a nice sort of way, for a Friday afternoon.

"Ladies here about Jimmy. They saw someone stealing the dog, they were driving a vintage car. They broke a house window, the one in the door," Billy summarised.

"If they've got a vintage car, why would they need to nick a dog?" commented Matthew.

"Breaking glass? That would've been noisy," said Liam, frowning at us.

"Policeman said they used brown paper and glue to keep it quiet," I chipped in.

"Well he would know. Any glue on the broken shards?"

We didn't know. No-one had said anything about glue on broken shards. No one had said anything about shards.

"Local, I reckon," said Billy, "otherwise how would they know about a dog worth pinching even being there?"

I hesitated then said, "The police think the thieves 'cased the joint' – looking around the area."

They looked at me then at each other.

"Yup, that's us alright, that's our Jimmy. Creeping about and looking for dogs to nick. When he's not studying for his college course or chasing girls. No wonder they only solve 2% of crimes. And why a dog? Not an easy thing to nick, they need feeding and looking after," Pearl wasn't impressed.

"Yeah, then buying a customised vintage car to drive it away in – that's just what he'd do!"

"What do they think we'd do with it anyway, a thousand-pound show dog?"

"Twenty thousand," I corrected. Billy blew out his cheeks and others raised their brows.

"They probably think we'd eat it."

They shook their heads in exasperation.

"Sell it?" I suggested.

"Who to? Who do we know with twenty grand for a dog? The police are so stupid."

It was a day for rueful smiles.

"The thieves took the dog at night though. So how could you see it happening?" asked Billy.

We explained again about the streetlight.

"Breaking into a house in bright light? Through the front door? Bit stupid. How did they know the family were away?" asked Matthew.

"They weren't away," I said, I felt self-conscious for some reason. "They were asleep upstairs."

There were frowns at this. "Did the house look empty? Was the milk on the step or mail piling up or something?"

"No." There had been no such unusual circumstances and I remembered something else.

"Their cars – two of them – were parked on the driveway at the time. So it was really obvious they were home."

Our new acquaintances exchanged looks.

"Breaking into a house, in bright light, to nick a dog when the family's home?" Billy summarised.

"Why didn't the barking wake them up?" asked Liam. "You sure they were home?"

Angela and I looked at each other.

"There was no barking."

"No barking? Dogs always bark when there's somebody home, when there's an intruder. Believe me, I've worked as a postie and a milkie – it never fails. Did they poison it then?" Billy queried.

I shook my head. "The dog walked to the car, it wasn't barking or whining. It was panting. It got in the back seat."

I remembered thinking that the woman was panting and that the white I could see was her skirt.

Matthew was shaking his head. "The dog knew the thief then." The others nodded or murmured consent at this.

"They arrested Jimmy but any of us would have done for them, they've got their nick. We all had alibis and Jimmy didn't. He was studying for his course."

"I knew no good would come of that!" said Pearl.

Billy and his mother exchanged a glare.

"Book learning! What good ever came of that, look where it's got him!" said Pearl.

"Better than——" started Billy.

"Drop it!" said Liam and there was both a plea and a warning in his voice. Billy and Pearl fell silent. There was a pause.

Liam said to Angela and me, by way of explanation, "Pearl is old school: doesn't hold with your language and so on."

"He means reading," added Billy, seeing our mystified faces.

Pearl's jaw looked set and she looked at the horizon.

"They said the dog was worth £20,000," I said.

"Only to someone who could sell it for £20,000," said Liam. "Someone already in the business, with connections. Anyone else would be shopped the minute they tried."

"She was pregnant – six puppies," I added.

"Okay, we're looking for someone who can look after a breeding dog and the puppies when they come and who can sell them on without being suspected. And someone the dog knows. With a funny-coloured vintage car. That's gotta narrow it down a bit!"

There was a pause.

"A puppy farm? It could be hidden in plain sight? What sort of dog is it?" Liam asked.

Angela shared a copy of the poster from her handbag.

"Not exactly your average mutt, is she? That would stick out a mile anywhere, all that white fur!"

"They could trim it or dye the hair," I suggested, thinking of my own various adventures with chemicals, boxes, and tubes.

"Then it would look a mess and who'd want it?"

"Are there any puppy farms round here? I'd guess in a 50-mile radius," Liam wondered.

No-one seemed to know.

"Da'll be home soon, he knows the area better."

They all nodded agreement to this.

"Da works the harvests in the area so he's travelled more around here. He's at the lambing now," Billy explained for our benefit. "We're usually all on nights at Felthams for the canning when we come here. The girls are mostly at the cafes for the season."

I nodded as if I knew what this all meant though I

hadn't a clue. I knew Felthams was a big factory on the other side of town but I didn't know what it factored or who did the factoring.

Pearl was pondering. "What colour is the streetlight outside your house?"

Angela thought for a second. "A sort of orangey-pink," she said. "Why?"

Pearl said, "Was there a moon that night? If the only light would have been the orange streetlight …"

Her elder son caught the thought and ran with it. "So not beige then? The roof is actually white in daylight and looked orange in orangey light but what colour goes beige in an orangey light?"

We all pondered this. None of us knew.

Billy said, "Hand me the lamp." Liam fetched an electric lamp from the tool box. Billy looked around, then at me, and held his hand out. "Your neck scarf would do."

I flustered until I saw what he meant and handed him my orange, patterned scarf. He stretched it over the lens of the lamp and switched it on. The light shone through the orange fabric. "Anyone got anything blue?" Liam opened his shirt to show a blue cotton T-shirt underneath.

"We'll have to use your van, Ma, 'cos the blinds work best," Billy and Liam went into a caravan and we saw black blinds being lowered in the windows.

"Only way to get you lot to sleep when you were bairns," Pearl muttered.

In a few seconds the men were out again.

"Yup, in orange light blue looks more beigey, a light, muddy colour. So, now we're looking for a light-blue or light-grey car with a white roof. Got the phone?"

Something was already ringing bells for me.

Liam pulled a phone, wrapped in a cloth, out of his shirt pocket, switched it on, and passed it to Billy.

He tapped into the phone for a while and held up the screen. On it was a whole raft of pictures of cars which were pale blue with white roofs. One of them in particular was one I had seen before.

Then I remembered where.

"The car in the film – the magic one!"

Billy, Liam, and Pearl looked more than suspicious now as they eyed me.

But Matthew suddenly laughed and said, "The Anglia! The Ford Anglia! The Harry Potter film!"

I had seen it on the cover of the DVD on the night I had brought it for our 'film festival' with the grandchildren. That was where I had seen it before.

The others looked at him as if the madness we'd

brought was infectious.

"It's a good film," Angela said defensively and Matthew nodded in agreement, delighting in the others' ignorance of such matters.

"Jimmy and my two went to see it and I went with them, great film. And a pale blue Ford Anglia, with a white roof!"

"A Ford Anglia?" Billy looked quizzically at the other two mechanics but they shook their heads.

"We haven't seen one of those in the garages here. Mind, we've only done a few day's work at them, but it hasn't been here for repairs either. We've been here a few weeks," he explained to us, keeping us up to speed.

Angela and I nodded. We could have told them the exact day of their arrival given the frenzy of the cul-de-sac's talking drums on that momentous day.

"Pity really, that's not as rare as the orange-roofed, beige wonder would have been. Still, I'll try a long shot," Billy said and took up the phone again. "I'm giving a shout out – the cousins might have seen something."

Liam explained, "We're a big family – lots of cousins are mechanics as well, all over the country. A lot have come off the road but there are others still travelling."

"You'd call them second cousins or third cousins but to us they're just cousins," said Pearl.

"I'll have the phone after you," said Matthew, "I'll ask my lot too."

Pearl was looking over Billy's shoulder at the picture of the car. She shook her head.

"That thing could never pull a trailer!"

"Anyway," added Liam, "our Jimmy wouldn't be seen dead in something like that – with or without a champion dog!"

They worked on the phone and pressed 'send'. Billy checked the signal and we waited.

There was a pause.

"Why are you helping us?" Billy asked, surveying us again with those eyes.

We didn't know.

"It just doesn't seem right," I offered.

They nodded in agreement.

"What you said at the meeting ..." prompted Liam.

"Yes, that," said Angela, she hesitated then said, "I've got a son and... grandchildren and ... people are horrible to them too ... their skin-colour ..."

She stopped speaking at that point and I realised she was upset. She was missing her son and his family who were so far away and maybe recalling that not so long ago she and I had also had certain beliefs about skin colour and it had cost her four years of the joy of being a grandmother.

Pearl didn't know all that but she heard the catch in Angela's voice and, as she was standing closer to Angela than I was at that point, put her hand on Angela's arm by way of comfort as if she did understand and Angela didn't need to say any more. Pearl gave Angela's shoulder a squeeze, communicating an understanding between parents and grandparents.

No-one asked for a more detailed explanation but several nodded sympathetically.

"You never quit worrying, do you?" said Liam, looking over to where the children were playing. "My two think they're immortal."

"They all do," said Billy, "mine too," and we watched the youngsters at their game, seemingly oblivious to the world with all its dangers and unfairness or the parental eyes that watched them with such concern.

"So did you at that age," said his mother.

There was a moment of resonance among all the parents present as we watched the children play.

We thought about Jimmy in his cell.

Matthew said, "If you were leaning out of the

window, did you hear the pane of glass being smashed? It might have just sounded like a crack or a bump? Or a thud?"

"You would know," said Liam.

"No, I didn't see her do that to the door at all," I said. I was quite certain of this now despite what the police, Charles, and Joan had all said, making me doubt my own senses. "I thought ... I know ... she went down the side of the house. She did go to the front door but I didn't hear anything being hit or broken. I'm sure of that now. Maybe we should go and see the police again."

"They'll want real proof before they'll look elsewhere, they think they've got their man," said Billy. I was to recall this too, how he didn't seem keen to go to the police with the new evidence about the car, even if it was only the evidence of my dodgy memory.

"Been many burglaries in your street lately?"

"No, not that we know of and I think we would know. It's a cul-de-sac, after all, "I explained.

"Mind you, we don't talk to each other much – to our neighbours I mean," added Angela.

They nodded at this and exchanged glances at this glimpse of our other world where people lived next to each other year in and year out but did not speak.

There was a silent interlude and we looked at the

common and the wind blowing the clothes on the washing line. One of the caravan doors opened and a young woman came out, pulling on a jacket. She came over to join us and stood by Liam with whom she exchanged smiles. Pearl brought her up to speed with why we were there and said to us, "Kathleen works some nights in the care home, the other lasses are at the factory or at cafes in town. I get to look after the kids. No problems today, love."

One of the youngsters ran over to see her mother and got a hug and a kiss from her and a ruffle of the hair from Liam then ran back to her friends. The young woman looked at me with a slight frown but then looked away without saying anything. I remembered her doing similar the night before and wondered what it was about me that puzzled her.

Then the phone pinged.

Billy looked at the screen. "Result!" he said exultantly. "It's from Jonah, he's near Derby now but he was west of here in January. They were camped near a place called ..." He peered at the screen. "Buttersville? They were mostly helping with some ditch-digging but then Jonah was temping at a garage he knows – works there some seasons AND..." he paused for dramatic effect, "he did a service and repairs on a Ford Anglia – blue with white roof! About two or three months ago. He remembers it 'cos it was in such good nick and he's a bit gone about vintage cars is our Jonah."

The others all smiled at this, they all obviously knew Jonah and his passions.

"Right," said Billy, "but Da's not due back until tomorrow with the car, we can wait until then to fetch more water and take the rubbish to the dump but this is urgent."

Matthew asked, "Who else has got a car that's working?"

Heads were shaken. "Da's has got my alternator."

"Still soldering the exhaust on this one."

"New carburettors won't be in 'til Monday."

"Hang on, what's the plan?" said Pearl. "We can't just all charge up there looking for this dog-thief. It's almost bound to be gorgers so who will the police believe? We'll be done for harassment. The dog'll be well hidden. We'll just be proving that Jimmy's part of a gang and make it worse for him!"

"We could find the garage, at least find where the car is, find the driver and look for the dog. If we can get the dog back the case collapses. Put it back in the garden, we know where it came from," said Billy, nodding at us.

"If these are professional dog-nappers the dog will be halfway across the country by now in a barn or a warehouse."

"But we don't think they are professionals, cack-handed professionals if they are. If they did it for a living they'd have a van and more dogs would be going missing and they wouldn't be breaking into houses where they know families are asleep upstairs. Or pinching a dog they know."

"So what else can we do?"

There was a silence. The children had finished their game and were sitting under a tree with the dog. He had been relieved of his clothing and was sitting, tongue lolling, among the children.

"Well, nothing without a car that's working," said Billy. "We can hardly rock up on horseback. We can at least go looking, so which one's nearest fixing?"

He turned back to look at the small assortment of old cars in various stages of repair and improvisation.

I heard Angela say, "Our car's working!"

I looked at her, so did everybody else, but I think I was the only one who was gaping.

Chapter Eight

Day Trippers

There followed a short decisive discussion about who needed to go and who needed to stay in case of: attacks by local nazis, unlikely in daylight, it was agreed, and even less likely now the biggest one of the fellowship sported a broken nose; visits by the police looking to arrest Billy and Liam more likely as there were warrants out for their arrest and they had already called once; the need for some to go to work later on, and, in case of finding the dog, the likelihood of the thieves being violent as well as incompetent which seemed very likely and necessitating the need for a little muscle on our team; the need to be back before nightfall in case of more 'trouble' – meaning visits by violent people in green jackets; the need to have enough people on site at all times to mind the 'bairns' and manage meals, all these considerations had to be factored in.

Matthew wanted to come on the trip but Pearl said, "No, I'm not choosing you for this one, not with your temper. This needs a cool head," which Matthew accepted with a nod as if he knew his shortcomings and strengths and that they were accepted by him as by the others as just part of what makes up a person.

The decisions made, the selected group headed towards our car. Messages were sent to Da to bring him up to speed. Billy and Liam were to come with us in our car. We, Angela and I, made the group respectable and less scary. They gave it strength. Both were features which might be needed. Matthew, Kathleen, and Pearl were to stay to mind the camp and the bairns until their jobs called them away; Siobhan and Fern – two sisters who had recently joined the band from another family – and Megan, Billy's wife, would be back in a few hours too, apparently, from various shifts and casual jobs. We headed towards the car.

Before we had gone half the distance, Kathleen called after us and ran over. I watched her, remembering what it was like to be able to do that, although only vaguely. She caught up with us but came over to me and spoke quietly. She looked at me and said, "You know, Simon isn't doing right by you. I thought you ought to know, you seem nice." She waited for a reaction.

I had opened my mouth but I didn't know how to respond.

Liam said reprovingly, "Kath, honey, there's a time and a place you know …"

She pulled a face at him and did not retract her statement.

Angela said, "You mean he's seeing somebody else?"

Kathleen nodded. Her work done, she moved away and jogged back to the caravans.

I still wasn't sure what to say. I remembered picking Simon up from his work at various jobs on numerous occasions, sometimes he'd be surrounded by his contemporaries and colleagues on some work project or other. I remembered the glances and smiles in my direction and the sometimes ribald remarks made for our benefit as he'd walk away from the group and get into my car. I wondered which of those groups had included this young woman and what else she knew.

Liam made himself busy, looking at the road map again to check the route. Billy busied himself looking at the horizon as Angela hunted for her keys and got the doors open.

"You okay?" said Angela as we got in, Billy and his cousin climbed into the back.

"Sure," I said, as nonchalantly as I knew how, "I've long suspected it. Apart from which," I realised, "I've never really 'done right' by him."

That was true.

"I mean, I always was 'seeing someone else' all the time I was seeing him – namely my husband."

"True," agreed Angela, and we set off for Buttersville. Liam and Billy seemed to find objects of fascination out of each of their windows as this muttered conversation was had and then, after a decent interval, they pointedly and delicately changed the subject as if they had heard nothing and, if they had, it was none of their business. Two very nice young men, I decided.

On the way, I pondered mine and Simon's relationship. From hot and steamy it had dwindled into merely exciting a long time ago, an exciting break from the mundane routine of married life. But more lately, now that Frank and I had parted, there was nothing much for it to be an exciting break from.

Further, it had always been good to be glamorous and illicit – the one with the smart car and the means to pay for the good meals and nice hotels, the wordly wise, the well-dressed, the femme fatale, the mysterious older woman who had lived a little. But sometimes wasn't it good to receive a response to some reminiscence of mine about a film or a gig of years ago that was something other than a blank stare? It was nice to be glamorous and well-groomed and to fascinate with witty anecdotes and observations but wouldn't it be nice not to have to? The affair was an escape from the routine and the everyday but now I was missing that routine and everyday. I was missing Frank and our comfortable, old-shoe life together, the no need for witty repartee and the comfortable silences of familiarity, the intimacy of long understanding …

Wait a minute … I was missing Frank?!

The shock of this brought me back to present reality with a jolt. The countryside was streaming past the window, Liam was navigating and Angela was driving. We were on our way to track down a gang of dog-thieves to 'spring someone out of the joint', if my recall of American crime movies served me correctly. Yes, I was missing Frank and our quiet afternoons by the pool.

It was an interesting journey. The country we travelled through was just fields and woods to us but to our companions it was a wealth of memories of previous camps, different jobs and employers, other travelling families, horses they had trained and encounters – some positive, some not with the non-travelling 'settled community'. They were both seasoned raconteurs and adept at entertaining others. I felt after a while that a road could be so much more than just something you drive along where fields and woods could be so much more than just part of a landscape you look at in passing. They could be places you actually lived in and belonged to.

We talked about the meeting. Billy was bemoaning the ruin of a good shirt as the nazi's blood had spurted onto it and stained a sleeve. "Blood doesn't come out in hot water and it had dried overnight with us sleeping on the common," he muttered. "Megan bought me that shirt."

"Yes," said Liam, "well you should have thought of that before belting that big skinhead in the face! When I break somebody's nose, I step aside lightly, like a butterfly, I don't stand there letting them gush all over me threads."

Billy couldn't help smile but retorted, "Oh yeah, you were being really careful with the one you were tackling, tipping that rubbish bin up and jamming it over his head!"

Liam retaliated, "He was lucky, there was a dog-waste bin right next to it but I was feeling charitable. Next time I won't be so generous."

I offered to be a witness against the charge of 'assault'.

"I mean, they did come after you and there were three of them. Plus they had shoved and yelled at us. We were quite frightened until they went after you two. Thanks, by the way, for taking them away."

"I thought they weren't going to go after you," said Angela. "They hesitated and seemed to discuss it among themselves when you had gone out of the door."

"They were probably trying to figure out if three is a bigger number than two," muttered Billy. "Not the sharpest knife in the box, yer average nazi! Thanks for that though. Good of you and those two with their petitions as well, they seem the right sort and Da's in touch with them. Four statements should make the coppers back off. They could charge those skinheads with wasting police time."

"Everything the police do is a waste of police time," murmured Liam. "They should be made to re-train as something useful: plumbers, roofers, litter-pickers, nurses, anything apart from being full-time professional pains in the a! Anyone want a mint?"

"Is it like that then?" asked Angela. "I thought they were all like *Colombo* until I saw the film *Billy Elliott*, I was so shocked!"

She described the difference; neither Billy nor Liam had seen either production, their television and screen time being somewhat limited living off the grid as they did but they drew on their real-life experience of the material under discussion and were able to assure Angela that the one representation was far more accurate than the other.

We learned of how so many Travellers had had to 'come off the road', their homes confiscated or the lack of sites making life impossible under new laws, and, where common land had once been widespread, all but 2% of rural land in the whole country was now closed to public use. We had not many places to go rambling or camping and Travellers had nowhere to live.

Billy told us of his police record; one winter there had been no work, he had been mending roads but the funding had ended. With a young family to feed he had shoplifted some basics from a local supermarket and been caught. The cost of the things he had stolen – mainly food – had amounted to about £20. He didn't know what the court case had cost. He had not been able to pay the fine, "You'd think they could have figured that one out," and he had done some months in prison.

"Nearly everyone in there was skint!" he said. "What do they do with all the rich shoplifters? And the forms I had to fill in! They asked me my 'ethnic origin', this little box I had to tick or write in! Well I'm Catholic, French and Irish by descent on my mother's side, and Jewish-Italian on my father's and I was born in Wales. You try getting that lot into one of those boxes. You'd better never get nicked, Liam, with your lot, they'd have to invent a whole new form."

"I'm pure Scouse," objected Liam, as if much offended.

"Do Travellers—?" Angela began to ask but Billy held up a hand to stop her.

"Any question that begins 'Do Travellers' is going to be problematic. Which Travellers, I'd have to say. It's like me saying 'do women' something or other, or do 'some other group' and you'd have to say 'some do, some don't'. I can't speak for all any more than you can."

"We all travel," said Liam, helpfully, "or would like to but we do all live differently. I'm the best. Billy here is not such a good example—"

"Horses are important to us," Billy interrupted. "So is family. We all know our second cousins which most gorgers don't bother with. We live with all the generations together, we help each other out, we fight too at times, we have rituals for sorting out disputes, so do you, but we don't have any people in wigs or uniforms presiding. We elect people to do stuff they're good at. We live outdoors mostly, we have our own languages, a history – mostly of getting picked on by you lot. That's about it, and there are different threads to the tapestry, different Traveller groups; my sister is with her husband's people who stay mostly around Scotland for example. We see her at Appleby most years. That's about it."

The drive to Buttersville passed quite quickly.

It was a satellite village centred around a bridge over a small river. It had a church, some shops, a pub, a garage, and houses. Angela and I were to head up the first part of the operation – some blatant respectability, we had all agreed, was more likely to oil the wheels of deceit than abrupt confrontation. I felt the same way I'd felt when skiving lessons for a quiet smoke at school but checked my grins of delight at seeing the seriousness on the others' faces and recalling that their brother was in jail and that they might follow if this went wrong. Kidnapping carries long sentences, dog-napping probably not so much, but conspiracy to pervert the course of justice, aiding and abetting, breaking and entering all hung in the air too and Jimmy was only 19.

A plan made, Angela and I left the car and walked over to the garage. I became suddenly aware of being very hungry and of not having eaten anything or drunk any coffee since brunch-time and of being full of jitters and withdrawal symptoms.

There was no-one in the office. We wandered into the yard. Cars were parked everywhere and one was on a raised ramp over a pit. A middle-aged man in overalls saw us, climbed out of the pit, and came towards us, wiping his hands in a familiar gesture on an oily rag.

He explained that 'Jeff' had just popped out and asked if he could help us. We didn't know who 'Jeff' was but guessed he was head honcho at the outfit. We explained the predicament we had cooked up: Angela wanting to buy my car but wanting more details about its history. I was to pretend to be the Ford Anglia's owner who had had the exhaust fixed as part of a service 'about two or three months' ago and wanted to check the date as I was now selling the car but the page in the record book had been spilled on and smudged so you couldn't see the date and Angela wanted the Full Service History and would not be fobbed off. Angela tried to look stern and resolute at this point which would have made me laugh out loud if I hadn't pinched myself quite hard. The story was thin but it was garbled enough to be true and tiresome enough for the mechanic not to want to know more but to take us into the office to fetch the big desk diary, put it on the counter, and start to open it to look back through the pages.

"Ford Anglia, you say? We don't see many of those. I think I remember it – blue and white?" I nodded as he ran his finger down the lists of dates, each of which had two or three cars pencilled in for various treatments.

"I expect Jeff booked you in, did he?" he said, conversationally. We agreed that he had. "I remember cars better than people," he added, then … "Ah, Ford Anglia, January 8th," he said triumphantly. "You're Ms Pederson then?" He looked at me, smiling. For a moment I had no clue what he meant but Angela said 'Yes' for me. Then she suddenly lifted her arms and stretched and yawned quite unreservedly where she stood by the window. The mechanic looked at her bemused at this uninhibited expression of exhaustion.

"Late night last night," muttered Angela, yawning hideously into her hand.

A moment later something made the mechanic look past us through the window and, with an annoyed grunt, he suddenly excused himself and headed out of the door in a hurry. We grabbed our chance and turned the diary towards us. We didn't just need the date, we were hoping that, like my garage, they'd write the phone number or address next to the appointment.

We could hear the mechanic talking to someone outside. We knew that someone was Liam – he'd been nominated to cause a diversion at Angela's signal to give us time and had been waiting out of sight for his cue. Because of his tattooed arms, earrings, and dyed turquoise quiff, we had all reckoned he'd be the one most likely to cause a distraction as anyone seeing him in the garage would assume he was up to no good and go and see to him, giving us a diversion. This had worked perfectly. I could hear Liam's voice, artificially slow, holding the mechanic in some conversation or other. We looked at the date – January 8th – the words 'Ford Anglia/Service' were written in pencil, next to it the name 'Pederson' and, most important, a mobile number then the word 'Cheltenham' and a big tick and 'paid' written in capitals.

I had a pen ready in my pocket and quickly wrote the long mobile number down. We turned the diary back and tried to look innocent, browsing the shelves of sweets and infinite varieties of oil on the mechanic's return. He didn't seem to suspect anything. "Bloody gypos," he said, for our benefit. "You can't be too careful with them hanging about. Now then." He looked up something on the laptop on the desk and obligingly provided a copy of the receipt confirming the exhaust had indeed been replaced on the date in question and gave me a stamped confirmation that the service had been completed and printed off a copy of the record of work done. Angela tried very hard to look interested as he translated the list of work done. He apologised for not knowing the car well or recognising me and explained that another mechanic had worked on it who, although very good, had only been a temporary and had now left. We smiled and left. We didn't tell him that the 'very good' mechanic who had worked with him was another 'bloody gypo'. There was no point in blowing cousin Jonah's cover in case he was back that way at some point and needed work again.

Pulling into a layby some distance away we dialled the number, or rather, Billy did, on my mobile on conference. Oddly, we heard the ringing tone begin even before all the numbers were dialled. Billy was primed to be 'from the garage' with a 'mix up about records and receipts' and wanting to check that 'we' had the 'right service record on the right car – at the right address', two Ford Anglia records having become 'mixed up.' It was hopefully vague enough to sound realistic to the majority of the population who know nothing and care less about how garages keep and manage their records.

The number gave an answering machine so Billy ended the call without leaving a message.

"He's likely got the garage's real number on his phone so he'd just call that if he got a message and we'd be rumbled. I'll try again later."

We all waited a while. We got out to stretch our legs and look around. Billy tried again a while later but it still only reached the ansaphone.

"I wonder why he brought his car all the way over from Cheltenham?" Angela speculated aloud.

"Why Cheltenham?" asked Liam and Billy together.

"It had 'Cheltenham' written next to the name," I explained.

"That's a long way away."

Billy had some hunks of bread and cheese in a paper bag and shared them out. I passed around the car's water bottle. We were each careful to pour the water into our mouths without touching the bottle. Covid's newest variant was never far away.

Then Billy said, "Maybe it's not the town."

We paused and looked at him, mid chew.

"Maybe it's a street." He saw our blank looks. "Cheltenham?"

"Cheltenham Street!" we said together.

"And those extra numbers … the phone number's too long, isn't it?" We consulted the long number we had scribbled down from the garage's diary again. The last two and apparently superfluous numbers were two and seven. We had assumed they were part of the telephone number but …

"27 Cheltenham Road – or Street. Right!"

We finished the bread and cheese, Billy tipped out the crumbs from the paper bag, folded it away to an inside pocket, and we got back into our trusty steed. I turned the car around and we headed back into Buttersville.

Chapter Nine

Glimpses

"Would this place be in an A-Z?"

"Too small. Might be worth a try."

A trip to a corner shop and a quick surreptitious peek in an A-Z of the region established that Buttersville wasn't considered grand enough for inclusion with its own map and also that the proprietor had not heard of Chelthenham Street. Billy bought a bar of chocolate by way of courtesy and we shared it as dessert as we pondered some more.

"We could ask people."

"There's a novel idea."

Asking the few passersby whom we encountered also drew only long, speculative silences followed by shakings of heads and apologies at best or a silent hurry away at worst. We were stumped again.

"Postie'd know," said Billy.

We found a red post box. We were in luck – the only collection of the day was still due, and soon. We waited again, wandering up and down the main street trying not to look suspicious. The town seemed to be mostly gift shops with a tiny mini market in the newsagents for anyone needing anything other than a souvenir. As a whole group of us might excite alarm, Angela was nominated to be the one to greet the postie and she waited by the post-box. Right on time, the red van pulled up, the postie got out, wearing the familiar uniform with her long hair in a pony tail, unlocked the box, and began emptying it into her sack.

Angela asked if she knew where Cheltenham Road was. The postie looked up, hesitated a moment then pointed, "Carry on down here, third left, second right, Cheltenham Road – Cheltenham Place is at the end." She went back to locking the post box, lugging the sack into the back of the van and driving off.

"Thanks," said Angela to the retreating van. We were on our way.

There were numbers 27 in both Cheltenham Place and Street.

"At least we're narrowing it down," said Billy.

We parked in a corner and took a walk along both roads.

"My money'd be on 'Place'," speculated Liam.

The 'street' had gardens, steps up to the front doors, bay windows, and the houses were semi-detached. 'Place's' abodes had only a concrete yard or two between door and gate with steps going down to basements and bins while every house had two numbers on the front. 27 had green curtains. 27a was down the steps and out of sight. We parked at the corner so we could watch both 'place 'and 'street'. It looked just like the kind of place a gang would hide out.

We checked for a back entrance and found a narrow path running along behind the houses. The tall wooden gate which was at the rear of 27, as far as we could make out, had been used recently, the weeds and grass being trodden down by recent traffic from the back of the house, but there was no sign of any dog in the small garden which we could glimpse through the slats of the gate. The path only led to the road at the front so there was no need to keep a separate watch on it.

We went back to the car to wait, trying again to be inconspicuous.

Time ticked by. We took it in turns to use the little path as a public convenience as there was nowhere else apparent and we didn't want to leave our position. I had often wondered how all that side of things worked during the 'stake-outs' I had watched on the telly.

Angela entertained us with chat about films featuring Travellers including 'Into the West' and 'Chocolat' and television's 'Jamaica Inn'.

She fell in love with a Traveller in 'Chocolat', she enthused.

"Sensible lass," said Billy, approvingly.

"And in 'Jamaica Inn'."

"Seems a bit of a theme. I'll look out for them. Thanks."

As the sun was getting low, and we guessed it was around teatime as the bread and cheese felt to be a long way away, a pale blue car with a white roof turned into Cheltenham Street, drove along it quite slowly, went past our car, turned into Cheltenham Place, and parked just outside number 27.

A thin man in a long, dark coat got out. His hair shone in the afternoon sunlight as he got a carrier bag out of the boot, walked through the gate, then seemed to spiral down into the ground as he went down the steps to 27a. He had glasses and sideburns.

"There's our man!"

"Basement flat. With garden. Could keep dogs there."

"He doesn't look like trouble, but you never can tell," speculated Liam. "Now what?"

"We go and ask him?" Angela proffered.

"'Oy mate, we think you nicked our dog', 'No I didn't, go away'. Yeh that would achieve a lot," was Liam's response. Billy gave him a glare and Liam mumbled an apology as Angela blushed under the sarcasm.

"You got any better ideas?" said Billy and Liam looked abashed. No, he hadn't.

We watched the house for a while. Other cars arrived and parked as the working day came to an end, the shadows grew longer and the permit-only spaces filled up.

"Well the dog's not in the house, he'd have brought it out for a walk if it's been in all day while he's been out," concluded Billy after ten minutes.

"So, what are we going to do?" I asked.

"Put the frighteners on him?" suggested Liam.

"Liam, beloved cousin of mine, could you step away from the more testosterone-fuelled solutions to problems for a nanosecond? He could go to the police and have us done with harassment. They'd love that – we're not exactly difficult to describe," was his reply, Billy looking pointedly at Liam's flamboyant coiffure.

"Anyway, how about we do like you said – go and tell him he was seen and could be in a lot of trouble."

"He'd rumble that, why haven't we gone to the

police already?"

We were stumped for a minute.

"I know, we don't want the publicity?" I suggested. That would be why I wouldn't go to the police, I thought. "We're reputable dog breeders and don't want to be linked with anything shady!"

"Good one. And we could say we just want the dog back alive. We don't want to panic anybody."

"But then all we'd be doing is warning them and giving them time to get the dog away and cover tracks. I expect that place is rented and he could leave without telling us anything."

"Whatever gang he's in, I don't think he's Mr Big of it," Liam pointed out, "looking at the state of this place! We could grab the dog when he comes out. He's got to take it for a walk sometime."

"Great, except it's a busy street. We don't know how many people are in there or nearby, there'd be shouts and barking probably if we tried that. If anybody sees us and describes us to the police, they'd know exactly where to come looking – then we could keep Jimmy company, charged with assault. It would give them evidence he's part of a gang, which is what they think anyway."

"Well what then?"

"We have to go and talk to him, we can't do

nothing. For Jimmy's sake. He's stuck in a cell while we're sat here."

"We could go and talk to him, we'd be less scary," I heard Angela say and I looked at her with a hard stare but she wasn't paying attention.

"True," said Billy, "plus you are gorgers so you'd understand each other. "

"Why thank you," said Angela, blushing red.

"Gorgers – not gorgeous – it just means you're not a Traveller," Liam explained, grinning at Angela's mistake.

"Not that I was saying you're not gorgeous," said Billy, gallantly, with a smile.

Angela couldn't get a deeper shade of red so she and I got out of the car. The two guys would watch for any sign of trouble from the gang in the house. I wrote out a text on my phone, addressed to Billy's phone, with only a touch of the button needed to send it on its way. I put my phone carefully in my pocket and kept my hand on it. If it looked like anyone dangerous was in the house we would not go in. If he reacted aggressively at the door we would back off.

We went through the little gate, down the concrete steps, and tried the bell. It wasn't working so we knocked.

After a short pause we heard someone coming and

the door opened. It was the driver I had seen at the wheel of the car – broad faced, red-haired, and bespectacled. He looked at us quite frankly.

"Hello?"

We realised we hadn't worked out what we were going to say as he looked from one to the other waiting for us to speak.

"I'm not religious at all, sorry," he said and began to close the door.

"It's about the dog!" blurted out Angela. I knew we hadn't agreed on what to say but I had assumed we had agreed not to say that.

He looked surprised and interested. Instead of pushing the door closed in our faces and running out of the back of the house or calling for his heavies to provide back up, or even reaching for a concealed gun under the long coat he was wearing, he said, "Oh right. You work with Anthea then? She and the dog okay?" with a tone of innocent concern.

I couldn't compute this and, by the look on her face, nor could Angela.

Without a second's thought I said, "No, we're private detectives hired by the dog's owners – who's Anthea?" And it was Angela's turn to look a bit surprised.

He looked shocked and then wary. The door began to close. "Well … she's not here," said our new

BEATRICE FELICITY CADWALLADER-SMYTHE

acquaintance, "and she's left … gone to London … took the dog with her … they're not getting it back."

He was edging the door closed, I put my foot in the gap. I'd seen them do that in *The Sweeney*, though probably not in open-toed sandals. I winced.

"Can we come in?" I remembered at least some of the script we had discussed in the car. "We don't want to involve the police but you could be in a lot of trouble!"

He looked alarmed at this. And surprised. "Why would we be in trouble?" he said.

His eyes behind the glasses did not look aggressive – they looked alarmed.

"Let us in and we'll explain," I said, in the way I felt a private detective would speak. He hesitated a moment and looked us up and down then pushed the door open wider for us to go inside, saying again, "Why would we be in trouble?"

Inside, the short hall was festooned with banners and flags of different colours and the bedsit room it led to was likewise decorated with scarves in red and gold, purple, green and silver, glass ornaments, clocks and wind chimes, a large dream-catcher, a sun-dial, and a heck of a lot of books. A standard lamp wore a black pointed hat with stars and crescents on it. My fears for the dog increased. Our host's long coat on closer inspection was black but with odd shapes outlined in silver emblazoned on it. What looked like a broomstick leaned against one wall and what looked like a giant egg-timer stood in a corner. My finger found the button on my phone in preparation for things dastardly.

Our host grinned at us but not at all manically. Rather his expression was of hopeful enthusiasm.

"Do you like Harry Potter too?" he watched us, looking around wide-eyed, "I love all this stuff. Love the books – changed my life finding them, and the films too of course!"

"Your car?" I said, speculatively.

He nodded. "My dad bought me that – wouldn't give me the money but … anyway, it was in a bit of a state but I got it fixed up bit by bit. Bit daft really, gets us to work … meant a lot to me … shows they still, y'know … despite everything …"

He was rambling now, speaking a bit too fast and tidying up as he talked, picking up items at random. I realised that he was scared. He picked up a brown paper bag from a pile and breathed deeply into it. He fiddled with his phone periodically as if looking something up.

"So you're a Potter fan?" I ventured, by way of calming the situation with small-talk.

Angela was walking about the room in a hunched

sort of way, picking up random objects and peering at them in a manner I imagined she thought detectives employed but which was only annoying me and making our new friend nervous.

He nodded, gesturing for us to sit down on a sofa-bed festooned with satin throws of various colours. There was a sort of kitchen behind a curtain and a rail with some clothes on it and a chair. It didn't seem to be the headquarters for any gangs, Mr Big or even any Mr Smaller Than Average.

"I suppose it's because I'm a red 'ead you know," he said, surfacing momentarily from the bag and speaking in short bursts. "Carrot-top, ginger minger, freckle-face and all that. Teased at school. Hated it. Dyed my hair brown when my mum let me. Made a right mess of it. That made them worse. I hated my hair. Hated me. But then Ron came along. And everything changed. The teasing stopped. Some even called me Ron. Other kids with glasses stopped being called 'specky' or whatever because of Harry. It was great. I owe a lot to those books. There they were – the Weasley brothers, and their mum and dad, Ginny, heroes all of them and hair redder than mine!"

Somewhat reassured that we were not in the presence of someone who thought his car could actually fly or who was deluded as to his own magical powers but just a literary enthusiast we somewhat relaxed.

"You've read them?" he asked.

Angela could meet him on this common turf although I had to defer. I listened to them exchanging notes at first then entering into a fervent discussion on whether the whole story could be seen as a huge analogy of the fight against the forces of the evils of racism and fascism – the idea of 'Mudbloods' and other oppressive insults to minorities and a fight for the right of everyone to be valued for who they are against all prejudice and hate, our need to unite against oppression no matter which house we had been put into and the choices we all made about who we wanted to be and whose values we chose to follow ... I whiled away the time looking around at the various wands and posters of magical characters, topped over the fireplace by one of the red-haired young wizard himself together with his more famous friend and the brilliant, bushy-haired witch and the tiny elf who had apparently saved them all with a quite different kind of magic that wizards did not even understand and believed inferior.

Angela, I knew, had never read the books but she could hold her own as she had watched the films and, to be fair, our host was so enthusiastic all she had to do was nod occasionally and risk the occasional reference gleaned from one of them.

Eventually, having put all that to rights, our host recalled why we were there. Our host took up a paper

157

bag from the small, folded pile by the door and again breathed into it for a while then appeared calmer.

"Why did you steal the dog?" asked Angela.

He hesitated. He took a few more breaths in the bag then said, "I was only the driver. I can't tell you about it – it's all a bit complicated. You need to speak to Anthea. Will you go to the police?"

"It was a very valuable dog."

"Well look, I can't talk to you about the dog. Anthea's not here. She's gone away. I can tell her you've called. Though I don't know why they've hired detectives. Do you want to leave a message? I would offer you tea but," he glanced at a clock – a golden one festooned with dragons, "I need to go out in a minute."

It was an obvious hint, although he had made no move to get ready to go out. Under his black coat – I could see now it was more of a cape complete with hood – he was still wearing what seemed to be his everyday work-clothes of an ill-fitting suit and tie in quiet grey which screamed at the wondrous surroundings in that fantasy magical room. It occurred to me how so many of us are one person at home and another at work and yet another in different situations: a world full of people, all pretending to be somebody else. I wondered who that somebody else was and whether they ever pretended to be us and whether I'd like them at all if we ever met.

"Okay," said Angela, which pulled me back to the present. She pulled a piece of paper out of her handbag and, pushing aside a few half-empty jewel-encrusted goblets, put it on the table and wrote her number on it.

It wasn't the plan we had agreed but 'winging it' had also been mentioned and somehow we didn't feel we were in the presence of a ruthless crook. It felt like we could trust him to at least pass on a message, plus he obviously was worried by our 'private detective' ruse.

We stood up to leave.

"Look," he said, "I need to tell Anthea you called. I'll send her a message; I've only got her phone number. She doesn't live here anymore and I don't know her new address, somewhere in London. She could send you a picture of the dog so you know she's alright? That could be enough?"

"The owners want the dog back," I said. "But," I decided to bluff, "we'll hold off from going to the police for a day or two."

"Here," said Angela, digging in her handbag, "You need to see this." She opened up the folded newspaper with the front-page article about Jimmy's arrest and put it on the table. "Can you get this to Anthea? This is why you are in trouble!"

He looked at the headline and pictures, looking scared again. He dug in a pocket, took out a brown bottle, and swallowed what looked like a capsule from within it.

"Sorry about all this," he said, indicating the brown paper bag in his one hand and the small brown bottle in the other. "With the Paras for years, now I jump out of my skin at the slightest thing."

We left the little room.

Out in the corridor there was another door with a Yale lock, it was painted deep yellow and had a large 'A' on the door in the shape of a decorative flower. At the bottom of the door there were scratch marks in the paintwork. As we reached the outer door Angela nudged me and nodded towards some hooks at the back of it. Hanging on the middle one was a bright red coat.

Chapter Ten
Another Incident

"I don't think she's gone to London," Angela muttered quietly as we climbed back up the basement steps and onto the street. We could see Billy and Liam keeping watch close by, ready for trouble from a desperate dog-thieving gang.

"Private detectives?" Angela queried as we walked back to the car with our companions.

"Best I could think of. Bit of a threat but not too much."

Our companions considered the ruse had been a good idea as it offered us some protection and gave an excuse for the visit without giving away who we were, in case *he* went to the police.

"He seemed just a genuine guy, bit eccentric, bit keen on wizards for someone his age, mid thirties I'd guess, but not harmful. Nice guy. He said the woman, Anthea her name is, has gone away and lives in London. But her coat's still there and I think she lives in the next flat."

"Different coat? Don't gorgers have a lot of coats?" asked Liam.

"Not all," I said, thinking of my own bulging walk-in wardrobes that lined the walls of my erstwhile home, the one with the pool which I was beginning to miss.

"Maybe."

"Do you think it was a lie, about London?"

"Probably. We left our number. He did seem scared about the police being involved and said he'd ask her to ring us and tell us what's happening, whatever that means."

"Any sign of the pooch?"

We shook our heads. "Some scratches on a door but they could be old."

"He seemed surprised they could be in trouble, which was weird. It was as if he didn't know he'd driven a car where his friend went into a strange house at night and came back with a dog."

"And all that with the paper bag! What was all that about?"

"Panic attack," I guessed. "It looked like he has them a lot, pile of paper bags at the ready. He was quite scared of us! Just as well you two hadn't showed up or he would have gone into a coma."

We talked about our strange visit for a while but could produce no further clues.

The threat of the skinhead attack on the camp had not vanished and they were needed back home. Also, if the dog had been taken to London it was pointless trying to pursue it. We had to rely on the strength of his contacting her about 'detectives visiting' and see if that brought a result. There seemed good reason to think a gang was involved because, otherwise, why a woman from London would engage a friend to drive her to pinch an expensive dog remained a mystery.

The drive back was quieter than the drive out had been. I think we were all dispirited at the result of our efforts.

"At least we found the car and the driver," said Liam. "You *could* go to the police with that, it backs up what you saw that night and now you know the address and the car registration! "

"Oh, I didn't—!"

But Billy held up the brown paper bag with a registration number written on it and passed it to me.

"They could run a check on that and find some answers," he said.

"And we might be able to persuade the police to

take another look," Angela suggested.

Our two companions did not look optimistic. We fell into silence on the way back, each in their own thoughts.

On the way, the phone, which seemed to be a shared item, rang. Liam took it from his pocket. He checked who the caller was and handed it to Billy. "One of yours," he said.

Billy took the phone and spoke into it, "Yes? … Yes, that's me. Yes okay …Yes that'll be okay. See you then. Thanks," and ended the call.

"Got work for tomorrow," he said to his cousin. "Back on the vans – they've had a lot of sickness there this week."

"It's all that breathing bad air," said Liam.

"We do have masks, it's too hot to wear them though but it's money."

"What do you do?" asked Angela, by way of conversation.

"All sorts," said Billy, "is there a job we don't do? Only casual and covering for sick folk – all over the place. Half the time I don't know what I'm doing one day to the next. Still, it keeps me out of mischief."

"You must be doing something right if they keep calling you back," said Liam, "I'm off 'til next week with the place being closed."

They talked awhile about jobs and income and places opening and closing and which were the worst places to work in. They both nominated 'working with the black stuff' as the worst. It seemed that road-mending had used to be a regular source of income but that pot-holes weren't mended so often now due to 'cutbacks' which meant they had had to look elsewhere. They had to change what they did as the economy changed.

Then we had to stop for petrol and I got us a sandwich each from the cooler.

Then, quite suddenly, standing in the queue to the till and not thinking of anything in particular, it struck me what Billy had just said and its implications.

Back in the car, I looked at him in the rear-view mirror as if adjusting it before starting the engine but he looked quite relaxed, opening his sandwich and showing no sign that he was aware of what he had disclosed. I looked at Angela and she too seemed completely oblivious. We set off again and headed home, the horrible idea growing and developing in my mind.

As we arrived back at the site to drop off our companions, we saw Matthew looking out for us. He limped toward the car as we pulled up.

It seemed the police had been there – calling after

we had left – looking for Liam and Billy as they had half expected would happen since the nazis had gone to the police, reported assault and given their descriptions.

"Then they looked all around the camp, said they were looking for stolen goods. They took away a whole load of the clothes saying they 'looked stolen'. They took a lot of the kids' stuff too and some of ours that Pearl was in the middle of sorting."

Billy swore under his breath.

"The kids'll have to miss school again if the uniforms are gone. It wasn't 'assault', if we *hadn't* given them what for they'd have come here that night with god knows what happening." He looked at us. "A gypsy site got firebombed last winter. People lost their homes, lucky no-one was killed. Kids were asleep inside. Would you still be prepared to say what you saw at the meeting – that they started it, they came after *us,* not the other way around? The police will listen to gorgers." He smiled. "Especially gorgeous gorgers."

Despite my recent realisation about Billy I had to join with Angela in smiling at this and confirmed that we would. Angela said, "Definitely."

It was true. We had all seen the skinheads run out of the hall after Billy and Liam, we had been pushed and felt threatened by them too. We had all heard what one of them had called them. We had seen it was three against two as well. We had all felt afraid of what was going to happen and relieved when the three thugs had run out of the hall after Billy and Liam.

"Thanks," he nodded. "In that case I'll go down there and give myself up and explain what happened. Can I give them your names and addresses as witnesses then? If they know some gorgers saw it and will stick up for us then they'll drop the case."

Angela wrote hers down before I could find a way to stop her. With my recent insight I didn't want Billy to have our address but it was too late, the paper was handed over.

"And others there would stand witness too," Angela said. "Those two with the petitions."

"Oh yeah. I'll call and see them." He looked thoughtful, as if not used to support from such quarters. He glanced at the paper, "Honeysuckle Close? Oh that's quite close by, isn't it?" he said, and put it in a pocket.

I felt my suspicions were further confirmed as he somehow knew our road. Probably from advising his associates of where choice pickings were to be had.

We got in our car to leave. I called out to him, "We'll call you if we hear anything."

He gave us the thumbs up as he moved away,

calling, "Right, I doubt you will, but if Leon rings, you let us know."

"Who's Leon?" I said as we headed the car up the track and I struggled to get it into third.

"Don't know," said Angie, rooting through the glove compartment for sunglasses, "must be the wizard guy. We didn't ask his name! Some detectives we'd make, huh?"

I finally got it into third but hit the brake as the realisation hit me and the car stalled. I turned to look at Angela who had found the sunglasses and was trying them on in the passenger mirror.

"So how come Billy knows his name when we don't?" I said. That got her attention.

I could see her mind whirling, trying to come up with a scenario which would make Billy innocent but there wasn't one. Billy knew our wizarding acquaintance and the mysterious 'Anthea'. We had been set up.

It confirmed all my suspicions. The trip to Buttersville – a diversion – warning Anthea to get away and delaying us going to the police, giving his associates time to get rid of the dog. It was all part of how he, and probably Liam and maybe the others, operated. They had jobs, they had admitted, which took them 'all over town', putting them in prime positions to spy out the land and look for likely targets and things worth stealing. They had spotted the valuable dog and the dodgy window and alerted their associates. They had come unstuck because of my eye-witnessing the operation and because of the police arresting Jimmy, but they wouldn't be able to hold him because there was no proof, precisely because Jimmy hadn't done it. It was his brother and his network, but he would never tell on them as Billy very well knew. So the police would waste their time with Jimmy while the crime was covered up and the dog sold, until they had to let Jimmy go from lack of evidence and the trail had gone cold!

I explained it all to Angela. No doubt the wizard guy, Leon or whatever his name was, was busy clearing out of the flat as we spoke, having won some time for the gang and put us off the scent and was moving to another 'safe address', getting rid of the car, until the next time he was required for a 'job.' No doubt they *did* know people they could sell the dog to for thousands.

She didn't seem to follow it very well. I think she found it hard to see Billy in a negative light because he had called her gorgeous so I let it rest. I would wait until yet more evidence presented itself. I only hoped Anthea would be scared enough by our private detective bluff to tell all about Billy and the gang to save her own skin. Then we could go to the police with the whole story, the car registration, descriptions, and the address in Buttersville, and they would do the rest.

We arrived home, speculating about whether our red-headed acquaintance had yet got in touch with the mysterious Anthea and whether she would contact us soon and whether he had the means to scan the newspaper report to her – wherever she was.

Too hungry to wait for a meal to be cooked or delivered, we were fetching the coffee and Angela was opening a new packet of Bourbons when there was a ring at the doorbell. I went to answer it as Angela was getting out the cups. On the doorstep was a man who could only be a plain-clothed policeman and a policewoman in uniform. They both looked very serious and dour.

"Can we come in?"

They both showed me their ID cards and I invited them into the living room.

The policeman said, "I'm afraid there's been a murder …"

There was a slight pause after these words fell into our lives. The officers' eyes flickered as they looked from one to the other of us to register our responses.

Angela went white in the face as she stared in disbelief. I knew that, like me, her thoughts had immediately gone to those she loved best. She sat down suddenly on the nearest chair, staring at the policeman as the coffee cups hit the floor. We were both afraid to ask. I hadn't thought of my grown-up children for a while but it was their faces I saw first, then Simon's, then Frank's: Frank's face looking surprised to be included. But the policeman hadn't even finished his sentence and went on, "Your next door neighbour, Fitzsimmons—"

The relief must have hit us both at the same time but I managed to suppress a cheer and said, "Oh my god! Mr Fitzsimmons? But we were only talking last night." I saw the implication: we might have been the last ones to see him alive. My mind reeled.

"No, *Mrs* Fitzsimmons. He was away, she was on her own in the house. Of course, as spouse he was our first suspect but he has a solid alibi — at a surprise party at a hotel with golf club colleagues fifty miles away by train, thirty witnesses at the party, railway personnel confirmed his catching that particular train. The party went on with drinks in the bar until well into the early hours and he stayed overnight at the hotel. Night-watch staff and CCTV footage all check out and confirm. It couldn't have been him. She died sometime between about 7 p.m. last night and about 2 a.m. this morning. She was out walking in the garden and surprised a prowler, she was killed with blows to the head. We are here to ask you a few questions to clear up a few loose ends and to let us know your movements last night."

I fetched more coffee and put a plate of biscuits on the table. Angela fetched salt and covered the coffee spilt on the carpet. The police waited patiently.

The police could not tell us any more details other than 'the body' had been found by the milkman this morning who had called at the house. He had gone around the back because the recycling bags had been still outside and been blowing into the road. He had collected them, dropped off his milk delivery at the front door as usual, then taken them around the back of the house to put them safely out of the way and made his terrible discovery.

Together we were able to tell what little we knew: Mr Fitzsimmons had left the house – we were able to give the time as he had been so anxious about the train – we hadn't seen Mrs Fitzsimmons but she had called him from the back garden just as he was about to leave and so that must have been about 6.15. They'd been gardening all afternoon.

The officer's pen moved quickly across the page, writing as we spoke.

"If I write a statement of what you saw, you can both sign it?"

We agreed.

"What was he wearing when you saw him?"

I thought for a second.

"A suit, pale brown – brown shoes, shirt and tie, brown tie."

"Did you notice anything unusual about it, any marks? Or on his hands or face?" the policewoman asked.

I frowned, then realised they were asking if we had seen any blood on the suit!

"No nothing," I said, horrified at the thought.

"It was quite clean?" the two officers asked, glancing at each other. They nodded and one made a note in a small book. Angela looked bewildered.

"Yes," I said, "no marks or anything. I suppose there would have been a lot of …?"

"Blood, yes, there was. Sorry but we need to suspect everybody until we are sure who did it. That's why we're here."

"We were away all day," blurted Angela. "And we were at the meeting last night – lots of people saw us there. It started at seven. We walked there."

The police both nodded and explained why they had called. "There is nothing linking either of you or Mr Fitzsimmons to the incident, but we do have a main suspect. That is why we're here."

The police had already checked out Mr F's alibi and made an arrest. They were needing a statement from Angela to break the suspect's alibi. The suspect had totally denied having anything to do with murdering Mrs Fitzsimmons and had stated quite clearly that he had not even been anywhere near our close for the best part of a year. But he had admitted that he *had* been a regular visitor here before that as he had had regular work here. Everything pointed to him. She had been murdered in her garden, a garden implement had been used, a heavy electric hedge-trimmer as it happened, and he admitted to having worked here … as a gardener. He had also admitted to what Mr Fitzsimmons had told the police; that the Fitzsimmons had been material in losing him work in several other houses in the area – which gave him a motive. The man who had been arrested was Jake.

Mr Fitzsimmons had seen a man in the close 'answering to Jake's description' the day before the murder. His wife, Edith, had told him that Jake had called at the house asking for work and they had 'had words'. He knew his wife and Jake had crossed swords before as she would not take him on as a gardener and Jake had reacted badly to that several months ago. Mrs Fitzsimmons had also previously persuaded several neighbours not to employ him and no doubt he had got news of this.

"Where you can help us, ma'am," said the policeman, winding to a conclusion, "is by confirming that you saw this man, Mr Jake Kingston, only a few weeks ago in this close. He swears he has not been here for many months but if that was a lie and he *was* here a few weeks ago, that shows he is lying about that."

Angela gaped. I think I did too. We both knew what the lie was: Angela covering up the presence of her grandchildren by inventing a fictitious visit from her ex-gardener. She looked at me, then at the detective.

"No, I didn't see him," she said.

The policeman frowned. "See who?"

"Jake – I didn't see him in the close a few weeks ago."

"Mr Fitzsimmons told us that you did."

"Yes, I told Mr Fitzsimmons that I had but I hadn't – I was mistaken."

"You didn't see Mr Kingston?"

"Yes, no – I didn't."

"You saw somebody else? Someone who looks like him?"

"No, I didn't see anybody."

The policeman leaned forward in his chair a little.

"You do know that lying to the police is a criminal offence?"

"Yes but I lied to Mr Fitzsimmons, not you."

The policeman looked at her for a moment, up and down.

"Is there any reason why you would be protecting this man, Jake Kingston, ma'am?" He raised his eyebrows and kept them raised.

"No, nothing like that," Angela flustered at the inference. "No, not at all."

"You're recently divorced I understand?" he went on. He had obviously been in the close for five minutes and had been brought up to date with the news of the world.

"Yes," said Angela, blushing under his stare.

I felt we were heading into dangerous waters and that some things were more important than others. I realised that if the police thought Angela had seen someone else answering to Jake's description, they might go and arrest some other poor sod with black skin who happened to be passing the area on the strength of that – so I intervened.

"Angela had some visitors staying," I intervened. "They were people of colour. Mr Fitzsimmons was curious about them. Angela didn't think it was any of his business who her friends were, so she told him a little lie, that they were Jake's family. That's all." Angela looked at me. She looked grateful. The policeman's eyes narrowed.

"Your neighbour said Mr Kingston called at his house Wednesday afternoon and asked his wife for work and she turned him away as she had before.

They had words. His wife was found this morning lying dead with a head injury with the hedge-trimmer lying next to her covered in blood. Mr Kingston cannot account for his movements that night – he has no alibi we can rely on. We have retrieved the hedge trimmer and it is definitely her blood on it and cause of death. John Fitzsimmons said you told him that Jake had called here to pick up some garden equipment a few weeks ago, did that include a hedge-trimmer I wonder?" He obviously wanted to stick to the story he had heard first and had a good grasp of.

"But he *didn't* call here! I lied. I haven't seen Jake – Mr Kingston – for months, nearly a year," repeated Angela.

"You and he are on first-name terms?" the policewoman queried, eyebrows up as well.

"Well, yes, he used to come here every week. We got to know each other ..."

All four official eyebrows went just a little higher.

"Right," the plain-clothed officer said, shutting his notebook and getting up. "So you're saying he hasn't been here for a year, that you know of. You lied when you told your neighbour that you'd seen him recently and you have no reason to be protecting him. Is that right?" He waited for Angela to confirm, eyebrows up again.

"Yes," said Angela, looking bewildered and not at

all convincing.

"Right," he said, "I'll put that to Mr Fitzsimmons and ask if anyone else might have seen our Mr Kingston in the vicinity recently or on the day in question, apart from Mrs Fitzsimmons of course, the victim of this terrible murder. Forensics are looking into it. May she rest in peace." He said this with a hard stare at Angela.

"Amen," we both said.

"This is horrible," said Angela, "we were only standing outside with the recycling bags and talking to Mr Fitzsimmons and heard her call to him from the garden – that must have been about 10 or 20 past six last night!"

"Thank you," said the police officers. "What did she say?"

I didn't like to admit that I hadn't been paying that much attention but Angela replied, "She asked him if he had his packed snack with him. She was very caring that way."

"And did he?"

"Oh yes, a plastic tub full of sandwiches. Yellow with a white lid," she said.

"He didn't go back through the gate to get them?" said the policewoman.

"No," Angela was clear on this point, "he just got

in his car and drove off."

The police nodded and got up to leave, having made some more notes.

Angela walked them to the door.

"Thank you. We will need you to sign a statement about what you've told us. The house next door is a crime scene now so he has moved to a hotel for the time being," they informed us and left.

Later on we did take a closer look and saw the black and yellow tape strung across the top of the driveway, the front door, and the garden gate which also had a large, new padlock on it.

"That's horrible," we agreed. "Jake's arrested, Mrs Fitzsimmons murdered!"

"Jake wouldn't do anything like that," said Angela.

I thought of how personable and nice Billy could be and said nothing. I had only seen Jake in Angela and Martin's garden a few times during coffee mornings and only knew he was a good gardener.

We took showers, got takeaways delivered, and put our feet up to watch *The Curious Incident of the Dog in the Night-Time* but at about 8.30 the doorbell rang again.

It was Geraint the reporter.

Chapter Eleven

Lunchtime

We invited him in and we sat in the living room. He apologised for knowing our address but he had looked at the petition when Angela had dropped it in the hall after being pushed by the thug. He hoped she didn't mind and was she free for dinner? In her dressing gown and slippers and mid way through her Tikka Masala Angela was free for a lot of things but a dinner date wasn't one of them, except perhaps at one of the less formal establishments. He also said he had got my message objecting to his report in the paper and wanted to explain.

We gave him a quick update about the murder next door. It still hadn't sunk in that something so terrible had happened so close to us and to someone we knew, however slightly. Geraint sat forward and opened his mouth to ask questions but then looked at

Angela who was still looking shaken and fragile, and shut it again then said instead, "Sorry to hear that. You okay?"

"I expect it'll be quite a scoop for you?" I prompted.

"Not tonight," he said, "I'm off duty." Then he asked about the film we were watching.

I liked him better, despite his mis-reporting about the public meeting.

Over a cup of coffee he told us he wasn't the editor. He collected, wrote, and sent in the raw material about events in the area but what was done with it was out of his hands. "That's a poor excuse," I said, one eye on the television screen and soaking up dopiaza sauce with a piece of naan. "You still put your name to it."

He said, "Of course I wanted to be a Jon Pilger or a Paul Foot when I went into journalism but they don't do that kind of journalism any more. Apparently it doesn't sell. Scandal and venom – they sell. Truth is no headline grabber. The editor's got an angle to put and that's what carries the day. I do have to pay the bills. It was rubbish, I know, but I thought you were great speaking up like that."

He looked at Angela and I realised why he had looked up her name and address on the petition and that he hadn't really called to talk about journalism.

Angry messages left at newspaper offices seldom get the response of a personal visit by the complainee.

"I wish I could do something real for a change," he said, "I don't recognise half my stuff by the time the editors have finished with it. You go to a lot of campaigns?"

He told Angela more about how he had been impressed with her standing up at the meeting and speaking out. What was it she had said about her grandchildren? I had coughed at this point and set down a couple of cups of coffee rather firmly between them. Angela had looked up at me after this uncharacteristic loudness on my behalf and I mimed at her with my finger on my lips to keep schtum. I was very mindful of who this man was and what he might be capable of doing with his typewriter or word processor with information about someone else's private life. Angela seemed to cotton on and sipped her coffee, looking at Geraint with freshly suspicious eyes.

"Do you have grandchildren?" she asked to deflect away from herself. I was impressed with her dexterity but from there they moved onto discussing Skype meetings with family, then to online courses, and from there they discovered they were on the same Film Appreciation 101 course. They became immersed in debate about whether their latest assignment 'comparing the works of any two directors in the Film Noir genre' was as interesting as its predecessor, 'comparing narrative devices', and discussion of which films they had each chosen and why. I listened a while but as Geraint didn't seem to be wanting to pry anything too personal out of Angela with which to enchant the local area with a banner headline and exclamation mark on the following day's epistle, I murmured something about putting my feet up and sidled out of the room back to my takeaway, leaving them to talk.

I also wanted to check my phone as it had pinged a couple of times.

One message was from an unknown number. It was a woman's voice: speaking low and quickly, almost in a whisper. She said, "Hello, are you the detective? Leon sent me your message. This is Anthea, I'm at work. I can't use the phone, not allowed all weekend – double shift. I'll call as soon as I can, I finish on Sunday. I need to explain. Please don't go to the police. I'll sort it out."

If she was at work, where was the dog? It was good to have heard from her anyway. I was a bit surprised actually. I had thought if she had skipped to London that would be the last we would hear of her or the dog. There was something very sincere in her voice and it was a real plea for us not to involve the police. She didn't seem to know they were already involved and that a young man was arrested and in prison.

The second message was from Simon.

"Hi Beth, I need to speak with you, please ring – Si."

Beth. Not 'Honey' or 'Poppet' or one of the other cutesy names I let him use on occasion, just Beth – my proper name. 'I need to speak with you'. Yes, and I knew what about. He obviously didn't know he had already been rumbled. I wondered how the young Traveller woman, Kathleen, knew of his carryings on. So, he had met somebody else, probably a while ago judging by the cooling off in our own relationship and he was now going to do the right thing and tell me and 'dump me' which I think is the right parlance a la mode. Well, he can sweat awhile. I had no interest in having an affair with someone who was having an affair, and even less in being the dumpee rather than the dumper. I should have ditched him years ago, of course, but he *was* one of my nicest bad habits.

I didn't reply to either message but reheated my takeaway and had a glass of wine in the hardly ever used dining room, listening to the sounds of conversation still going on in the living room.

Half an hour later Geraint was taking his leave and I learned that lunch the next day at a cafe near his office in the centre of town had been agreed on between them.

I felt quite protective of Angela, after all, she

hadn't had a date since before she'd met Martin and none at all during their decades together. Apart from which, husband-time doesn't count as dating in my opinion so she was quite out of practice. I also felt she might be quite vulnerable with all the emotional upheavals in her recent life and I had read enough tabloid 'news' to know what could be done with enough malice and poisonous intent by those who called themselves 'journalists'. The Traveller site issue was still rumbling on and Angela, speaking out in their defence, could well be used, in the wrong hands, to make her a target. She had told him what she knew of the murder but he said he wouldn't use it as it was still being investigated and newspapers can prejudice juries.

We didn't talk about her date except to arrange my giving her a lift, and company in case he didn't show, and pick up time in case he did as I could do some shopping while they lunched together and found out how much they didn't have in common which is the usual format for first dates. I kept catching Angie smiling to herself in a goofy sort of way but indulged her. It was about time something nice happened in her life and Geraint, if he wasn't some sleazy paparazzi on the trail of a story, did seem as if he might turn out to be something, if not magnificent, then at least nice.

The police station phoned later that evening saying they had had my phone number from a Mr William

Lewis for me to act as a witness to an alleged assault by himself and a companion. I explained what I had seen and that others could also stand witness that it had not been an assault at all but that they had acted in self defence. The officer sounded doubtful as he had read the report in the newspaper but I stuck to my story and gave him a statement over the phone. I found the contact details of the young couple off the petitions that were still in the kitchen drawer awaiting attention and passed them on to him too as further witnesses. I also said my friend, Mrs Angela Crawford, would also make a similar statement and that, yes, we would both be prepared to go to court and face questions on the issue. He sounded disappointed but said he would write a statement from what I had said and would I call the next day to sign it as 'Mr Lewis' would be released on the strength of it. I agreed. Although I now knew that Billy was guilty of organised petty theft and dog-napping, there was no need for him, or Liam, to be found guilty of something they *hadn't* done.

The Central Cafe was just what it said it was: it was a cafe and it was central. That meant it was tucked away in a very un-cosy manner under the town's only flyover between the council building and a roundabout that had been left behind when the bypass had been built in a part of town where everybody seemed to be trying to get somewhere else.

Some effort to plant greenery outside the cafe had achieved a tattered laburnum and a patch of muddy grass gracing its exterior, but the view from within was mostly that of traffic heaving past, its main appeal being the double glazing's effects on the relentless noise of passing cars and ability to shut out most of the fumes in between customers' reckless openings of the doors to get in or out. After a quick stop at the police station to read and sign statements, we drove to the cafe, parked at its back, went in, and found a table. There were laminated menus on a wooden stand on each table, which seemed entirely superfluous as you could quite easily discern what delights were cuisine of the day merely by breathing in.

A young woman came over with a note pad to take our order when I noticed she was staring at me. There was a moment of sudden mutual recognition – from the Travellers' site, around the campfire on Thursday night. She glanced around her. "You don't know me, okay?" I nodded ascent. I was getting used to the fact that Travellers, to survive, had to hide who they were more than most. She got a cloth from her apron and wiped the table. "You might want to know, my sister will be here for her shift in a minute and Simon usually comes with her on a Friday if he's not got work." This was said in an urgent whisper. I nodded to show I had received the warning and she went away to get our coffees. At least now I knew what this young woman and her friend, Kathleen, had been whispering about at the camp site that evening.

Angela said, "Is there going to be a scene?" and I couldn't swear to it that there wasn't a note of eager anticipation in her voice as she said it.

"Not at our age, dear," I said, "besides, I've had my four years' worth out of him. If he wants to move on, who can blame him? We were never going to get married and settle down, were we? Kind of her to warn me though."

"You were never in love with him, were you?"

"No. It was *grande passione*! A fine affair!"

"Ooh, 'and now it's over.' That's from *Cabaret*!"

"No, it's from my life," I murmured as our coffees arrived.

I told her about his message and wanting to speak with me.

At that moment the cafe door opened with a swell of noise and fumes which ushered in Geraint, who saw us and headed over. Behind him the door opened again, almost immediately, and in came another young woman with long dark hair, looking remarkably like our waitress and, with her, Simon, wearing a high-vis jacket and work-clothes.

My peripheral vision told me Geraint had walked over to our table and sat down just as our coffees arrived but I was watching Simon with the young woman. They were talking to each other as they came in and did not notice me or, indeed, anyone else. They took a table not far away and their chat continued – lots of eye contact and smiles: a standard young couple who are fond of each other. Simon looked around for the waitress and I looked away quickly back to Geraint and Angela.

I hadn't yet made my excuses and left, as Angie and I had sort of half-planned in case Geraint did show up, and now he and Angela were deciding on lunch with Geraint looking to me to join them. Of course now was the time for me to decide to go shopping and leave them to tête-à-tête over cheese salads and a side order of chips, or whatever it was that people ate in these sorts of places, but I had changed my mind and took up a menu, ignoring Angela's surprised look and none too subtle slight jerkings of the head towards the door. Around the edge of the laminated menu I could still see Simon with his new love.

Geraint was saying this was where he came for weekday lunch-breaks when he wasn't looking for stories or drinking with likely sources in the nearby pub where people came to bend his ear. Angela was reciprocating with the qualities of her favourite haunts and eating places. I didn't take much part in the conversation and hadn't yet chosen a meal.

"'Cheese salad," I muttered, wondering how best to play this. The waitress came over again, glanced at Simon with her sister and looked back at me, biting her lip. Was she expecting a scene? I suppose thirty years ago I could have managed one, thrown a fit of rage and jealousy and pique, but, as you get older, apart from wanting to conserve energy, you do realise it is just part of life. Things move on, as do people. I could never have claimed Simon and I were ever 'in love': we had come to the end of a good four years of enjoying each other, that was all.

At that moment, Simon must have noticed a face looking his way out of the corner of his eye and turned to look straight at me. There was a quiet moment. Angela and Geraint both noticed my distracted attention and looked around. The young woman sitting with Simon looked over at me too, then at him.

I inclined my head by way of acknowledgement and he stood up and came over, excusing himself past a few tables on his way. "Did you get my message? I need to speak with you."

He at least looked a bit flustered I was pleased to see.

"That's okay, Simon, message received and understood." I raised my coffee cup to him and took a sip.

He glanced at Angela, said hello, nodded at

Geraint, then pulled over a chair and sat down.

"I wanted to tell you. I'm sorry."

"That's okay. We both knew it wasn't forever."

"You'll forget me."

"I'll give it my best shot."

There was a pause.

"Were there others?" I wanted to know, just for the record.

"No, none," he said, looking straight at me. " Just you, me … and Frank."

That helped. We managed to smile at each other.

"It was good while it lasted," I ventured.

He always did have a gorgeous smile. "You mean it was bloody fantastic!' he said, in a low voice the others couldn't hear. He always could make me laugh, self-conscious as I was now in daylight with its grey light doing nothing to soften my lines. His new love looked to be the same age as himself, in the full fount of youth. They looked good together. She was watching us and pretending not to. Her sister had walked over to her and was handing over her apron and notepad – they were obviously at tails ends of shifts and doing a handover. Our waitress left the cafe with one last look in my direction, maybe to check I wasn't about to attack her sister.

There didn't seem to be anything else to say.

Simon's new love came over, putting on her apron, then put her hand on his shoulder, looking at me, "I've got to go to work, hon," she said.

"Okay love." He held her hand briefly. "We're okay here. Fern, Beth. Beth, this is Fern." Fern and I sort of smiled and nodded at each other, both being gracious. Simon went on, "As well as that, I wanted to show you these photographs. "

I have to say I baulked a little at that. What photographs? My mind raced to various intimate scenes we had shared which had involved a camera on occasion and, panicking, I felt my face turn red in horror, staring at him in rebuke. Simon realised what I must have been thinking, shook his head quickly and held out his phone for me to see: his girlfriend leaned down to peer at it. Also, Geraint and Angela lost interest in their burgers and fries and leaned in too.

We all stared with bated breath as the phone displayed a series of photographs ... of a door.

It was a wooden door with brass fittings with a small glass square window high up in its centre-panel. I looked at it, then back at Simon.

"It's a door," I said, blankly.

"Not just any door," said Simon. "Fern and her sister are with the same group of Travellers as Jimmy, who's been arrested for stealing that champion dog. Fern told me Jimmy is small – he's only 19 so maybe still growing, but much shorter than his brothers. He's about 5'7 max and … look at this door."

It took a second to remember who Jimmy was and to realise which door this was … but it still just looked like a door.

"The Harrisons rang me to get their door changed," explained Simon. "They used that flyer of mine which you put out with your own – thanks by the way, that brought in quite a few bits of work. The door's window was broken, as you know, but it was cheaper than mending it to just to put in a new door. They had bought one. When I got there they just wanted it hung in place and the old one taken away, as quick as possible, but I took these pictures first. I knew Jimmy was supposed to have broken it and reached through to open the door and steal the dog – you told me that, Fern, but look at how high that window is. You'd have to be tall and have arms like an orangutan to do it. The Harrisons have got it wrong. Whoever broke that window, it wasn't how Jimmy got in. And another thing, it was reinforced glass and very small. It would have taken a pounding to break it. No way you wouldn't have heard that from where you were, Beth, just across the way, and no way they wouldn't have heard it either from upstairs." He stopped. Geraint reached over and took the pictures. We passed them around.

"And look," Simon took the phone back and flicked forward to another picture, this time of a window. "While I was there they also wanted me to fix a window in the side. It didn't close properly – swollen window-frame – they said it had happened in the winter rain but it had been like that for years, you could tell by the damage to the wood. It had been opened and closed a lot too, a gap at the top has damaged a lot. Look," he flicked again and there were close ups of a window-frame with tidemarks of dirt and exposed wood in one corner. There were also scuff marks of various ages on the tiled window-sill.

"They didn't see me taking these pictures. Again they wanted the work done cheaply and as quickly as possible, cash in hand – which suits me fine. But they were in a rush which made me suspicious."

"So … you think they stole their own dog and made the rest up?" I queried. "But I saw it being stolen."

"An insurance job?" suggested Geraint.

"That doesn't matter," said Fern, "it doesn't matter who *did* take the dog – or why – what matters is that this proves Jimmy *didn't*. He couldn't have done! They only arrested him because he's a Traveller and they reckon his mum, Pearl, isn't a good enough alibi!"

I remembered that my talk of an 'old car' might not have helped by pointing the police towards the Travellers' site but didn't want to mention that at this point. Nor did I want to say anything about Billy being the person most likely to have come down from the common one night under pretence of 'work' to have gone snooping about the expensive houses until he had found the dodgy window, spotted the valuable dog, and then phoned his friends in Buttersville. The plan had gone wrong – thanks to me – and his own brother had been arrested. The Harrisons might have taken the opportunity to pull a fast one on their insurance company by lying about how the thief got in but what we needed to focus on now was getting Jimmy proved innocent.

A presence arrived near to our table and made itself felt. It was the manageress and she wasn't looking too impressed with Fern's efforts so far. Fern straightened up, got out her notepad, and left the vicinity. The manageress gave her a hard stare which softened to a knowing look at Simon with an indulgent rolling of the eyes and a kindly, amused smirk to the rest of us the minute Fern had moved away. An uncomfortable thought occurred to me that she probably assumed I was Simon's mother.

"Their insisting the door was point of entry only means we can prove Jimmy is innocent of going in through the door but he could have used the side window."

"But they won't admit that because that means they get no insurance money – about £20,000. These photographs show it wasn't secure. Insurance companies don't like that."

"That's a bit sad for them, they've lost their dog AND they get no insurance money," said Angie.

"Bit sad Pearl's son's in the nick for something he didn't do," I hinted.

"Oh yeah! Let's just keep quiet about the window. *We* know Jimmy's innocent, the police can sort the rest."

I wondered if Anthea would be frightened enough to 'spill the beans' to the police about Billy. They would probably let her off lightly in exchange for information: she probably knew about a lot of the crimes and thefts he and the gang had organised.

We talked a while longer and came up with a plan. I walked Simon to the door on the way back to the car. He waved to Fern who was serving another table as we wended our way out of the cafe.

Geraint and Angela moved away to let us have a moment.

"You're moving on," I said. "Best wishes and all that. We had four years, we both need to move on."

"Thanks Beth. Now my dad has gone too, I don't

have to be a carer any more. It's been a long time, looking after them both. Glad I did it but I don't need to do that anymore. I don't need to stay here anymore but … I couldn't have coped with the last five years if it hadn't been for you. You lit up my days."

I smiled, accepting the compliment. "And my nights. Pleasure was mine."

"But now I want a relationship that's, you know, real, not just an affair and I'm going to live with Fern. We're going to be married, her family are quite old fashioned that way. I want what you have with Frank – or had, sorry – you know, being together and all that."

I didn't feel like telling him that I was missing 'and all that' as well lately.

"Married? Doesn't that mean a really big, expensive—?"

"No Beth, some rich idiots are Travellers, most rich idiots are not Travellers, most Travellers are neither rich nor idiots. I expect we'll have a small ceremony on a beach somewhere or in a wood, old-school style!"

"Her family accept you? Travellers, you know …?"

"I'm already learning Shelta, Fern is teaching me. They do the same work I do – bits and pieces, lots of mechanics and fixing things, recycling … we're quite alike really. Her parents have gone, they were both trapeze artistes years ago, Covid took them both but the rest of her family like me okay. I think it could work – they'll help us get a trailer."

"It's not an easy life, getting moved on all the time."

"I've never had an easy life. And I'll be with Fern. Plus it will be nice to see more of the world, all I've ever seen is this place and Bognor!"

"She looks great. I'm happy for you."

I suddenly felt tearful. This was Youth, with all its hope and reckless adventure. I'd visited it for a while, revisited it, but now it was goodbye. Probably forever this time. But the hard work of having to understand a twenty-something, cope with thrash metal, and explain what the 70s had been all about was also over, so there was relief too.

We shook hands.

We'd agreed to meet at the Harrisons' with the new evidence. Simon forwarded the picture and the video to my phone.

"Have you got the Harrisons' phone number? I don't want to be involved, working off the cards and all that." He left.

I gave the Harrisons' a call, saying that we had new evidence we wanted to share with them. Mr H sounded irritable.

So, at 5.30, Geraint, Angela, and myself rang the bell at the Harrisons' new front door. Geraint had said he would come along to act as a witness.

Chapter Twelve
More Details

Mr Harrison answered the door. He didn't look terribly pleased to see us and asked us what it was about before gesturing us inside where Mrs Harrison was arranging flowers. She didn't go into raptures either. "We're having company quite soon," she said, pointedly. They and Angela had never had been close but I knew, by the look she gave us both, that Angela's outburst at the meeting ensured we would never be considered 'company' in this house.

Just as we were about to speak, a police car pulled up outside. It was the officer we had met before, whom we had decided was PC Plum and who was presumably still in charge of the case. Judging by his expression he wasn't delighted to have to come and listen to our drivel again. I was surprised to see him there, attending to a stolen dog case, with a murder in the neighbourhood but noticed he and the Harrisons seemed on very good terms.

He spoke, "I hear you people have new evidence about the gypsy lad case? What's this all about?"

Mr H had poured out a drink in a short glass for himself and a glass of something else for Mrs H. We weren't included in this largesse, I noticed, as if we were on duty, like the officer.

I showed the photographs and explained about the height and about Jimmy's shortness of stature and about the thickness of the glass. Simon had photographed himself standing by the door to illustrate the difficulty. "He's 6'2," I informed them. "You can see his shoulder hardly reaches the window and no way is even his arm long enough to reach the lock on the inside. The suspect that was arrested is 5'6" or 7 at most."

"Who is that?" asked the policeman, pointing at Simon's picture.

Mr Harrison answered, "He's just a casual handyman, mended our door for us, working off the cards. Sorry if that is an offence employing him but I felt sorry for him, but now I think about it, he may well be another gypsy! He could easily have set up these pictures to look that way to get his friend out of trouble. It's all about perspective."

"Can I see the door to measure it?" asked PC Plum.

Mrs H explained, "It's gone to the dump. The window was broken and some of the wood was damaged. It was easier to replace it. It'll be crushed by now."

"Then this could be any door," said the cop, "photographs of any door."

I fiddled with the phone and showed them all the video Simon had also made. It began by the road sign showing 'Honeysuckle Close' and took us all along the road to the house number on the Harrisons' wall before finishing on the door itself with its broken window, with the measuring tape Simon had fixed by the side of the door showing its exact measurements and height of the window, as if he had anticipated the awkward questions. There was no doubt it was or had been the Harrisons' front door.

"Where did you get these?" said Plum, looking at the pictures.

"A friend took them."

"The same 'handyman' who was doing work on the house," interrupted Mr Harrison. "A shady character I reckon. He didn't do a very good job, now I know why. He spent all his time making up pictures! This isn't evidence!"

"True," said the copper. "These wouldn't stand up in court, he'd need to be cross-questioned and where is he?"

"But Jimmy *would* be in court and anyone could see Jimmy could not reach through that window to open that door. The jury would see that straight away."

The policeman looked uncomfortable. "Maybe he had a taller accomplice? He has brothers and they're all tall enough."

"They all had alibis that night. AND I saw one person going to the house and leaving with the dog. It was a woman," I said. For some reason I did not want to tell of our drive to Buttersville and the Harry Potter fan and his flying car or that the strange woman had flitted to London with the dog. None of that would help Jimmy

"He could have got in at the window!" blurted Mr Harrison, suddenly.

"What window's that then?" said the cop in a strange tone of voice.

"At the side …" said Mr H, his voice fading as if he realised he'd blundered somehow.

"Broke the door window then went in at the side-window?" The policeman frowned. "Doesn't sound likely does it? You didn't mention it before, did you?" There was an edge to his voice.

Mr Harrison seemed to retract. "No, it was locked and quite secure. It was just a thought, don't know what I was thinking. We are still very upset you know." He ran his hand over his forehead in a gesture I remembered from the meeting.

The policeman gave him a long stare then shook his head. "We haven't got a case. Not against this Jimmy person anyway. My inspector will sign the release papers. We'll check Jimmy's height and so on. You," he pointed to me, "need to tell us more about what you saw – or what you think you saw that night. This woman and what she looked like. You'll need to come down to the station and make a proper statement."

I nodded my assent.

"So we're no closer to knowing who stole my dog?" said Mr Harrison, ready to be angry. Mrs H went over to him and put her hand on his arm by way of comfort and, I thought, restraint.

"No," said the copper, "we're not. Have you heard from the insurance company yet? That isn't police business of course but it seems unlikely we'll be able to get the dog back at this stage as the first 24 hours are crucial in these cases. The trail's gone cold so my advice—"

"Yes, yes, it's all in hand," said Mr H irritably.

"And if there is a window that isn't *quite* secure that would make your insurance invalid, of course, wouldn't it?" continued the policeman, still looking at Mr H.

"Don't worry, it's perfectly secure," said Mr H. "All in hand."

Well it was now, I thought, now that Simon had replaced it, but I got the distinct impression that the policeman did not want the insurance company to find out anything about a dodgy window and wouldn't want to see the picture I had on my phone either.

"We can prove it wasn't Jimmy," I said, "that'll do for now."

We stood up to leave.

"We'll be moving those people on anyway," Plum said to the room in general, as we moved towards the door, as if to remind us who was in charge. "They're trespassing – they've outstayed their welcome."

"This is a *very* interesting story," said a voice and we turned back to see Geraint still sitting on the couch, writing in his notebook. He hadn't said anything during the visit and he hadn't even been introduced.

The Harrisons and Plum looked at him blankly.

Geraint stood up, put his notebook in his back pocket, held out his hand, and shook hands with the Harrisons and the PC.

"Geraint Wilson, at your service. Freelance journalist – reporter – from the *Gazette*. We've been following this story closely: dog theft; gypsy arrested;

meeting at the hall. I was there – very interesting stuff." He put his hands on his hips and blew out his cheeks, looking around at us, "Who would have thought it would end this way? Misplaced evidence, wrongful arrest, defamation of character, eye-witnesses not listened to, teenager taken from the bosom of his family and still no dog? That hardly ever happens, does it? Our readers *will* be fascinated." He rubbed his hands together.

The PC's face had fallen and so had the Harrisons' – they all glared at Geraint. I looked at Angela, expecting her to look as mystified as I was but she was looking at Geraint with a certain look in her eyes.

The PC glared at him.

"What do you want?"

Geraint walked over towards him. The policeman glared down at him. He was about a foot taller than Geraint and about a yard wider but it was Geraint who was somehow calling the shots.

"Just leave them be for a while, leave them be. They've done no harm. There's a petition out saying they're welcome. You can see he didn't do this. They'll be getting their son back. They've all been through hell, they could do with a break and I think there's a wedding on. Leave them be, until they move on anyway. They are Travellers, they do travel. Leave them be, then maybe this story won't hit the papers after all?"

"I'll want a guarantee!" muttered Plum, glaring.

"Okay, let them stay until they choose to go on. There aren't enough sites for them to live on but they have to follow the harvest and the work same as we all do. Their life is hard enough. And someone has to fix the cars and bring the harvest in. Let them live the way they do – the way they always have – doing no more harm than others do, probably a lot less. And the story doesn't get printed."

The policeman nodded. The Harrisons looked from him to us and back again, blustering, "That's blackmail!"

The PC coughed, "We call it extortion these days," he said, "and no, it's just an agreement between parties as to the best way forward. It *is* unjust that Travellers are not allowed to be Travellers and I stand by that. I might have been a bit hasty making that arrest, scared he was going to disappear, but now it's all come out that he is innocent, I see no reason why things should not proceed to a happy conclusion."

His sudden enlightened hypocrisy settled into the room and was most welcome by all except the Harrisons.

"What about my dog?" said Mr Harrison, "And you!" He glared at Geraint. "You pretend to be a journalist, a writer, but I notice you splitting your infinitives and ending your sentences with prepositions like there's no tomorrow!"

Geraint considered, "I think your similes need work. Also the ending-sentences thing is a rule for the Latin language, not for the English. The Victorians applied it to English because they wanted to be like the Romans in all things and have an Empire as big as theirs. But I'm not Victorian so I don't worry about ending sentences without prepositions nor splitting infinitives, nor do I dabble in the slave trade, court women in crinolines and corsets, or swan about the country in a barouche."

Mr Harrison gaped at him as the words hurtled past. He looked as though he'd like to hit Geraint, who stood smilingly benignly up at him. "Or wear a top hat," Geraint added.

Plum coughed to bring the conversation back to the issue in hand.

"I think," he began, "you will be properly compensated, Mr Harrison, as you seem to be adequately insured. It seems unlikely now that we will be able to find the real thief, though of course the case will stay open for the time-being with your neighbour's new evidence," he nodded at me.

The evidence wasn't actually that new, I wanted to say, it was just that he'd ignored it first time around on account of my story clashing with the Harrisons' own and my not being able to think of the word 'vintage' when I needed it and my being female and of a certain age, but I felt it to be undiplomatic to say so at this juncture.

"I think you'd better leave," said Mr Harrison with a cold edge to his voice which had not been there before when addressing the policeman, although we had certainly all had a taste of it.

"Would you like me to have a look at that window while I'm here?" said the policeman, helpfully and pointedly.

"That won't be necessary," answered Harrison. "There's nothing wrong with that window!"

I had a phone in my pocket with pictures which said otherwise but I kept quiet. We had to live opposite them after all.

"Well, I certainly hope not," said Plum. "The insurance would not be valid if there was, would it? Right, I'm off to release a suspect from custody."

Plum said nothing more, gave the Harrisons what can only be called a significant stare, nodded at us, and left. We heard his car start up and drive away.

He hadn't been acting much like PC Plum after all but maybe it was good for children to learn that looks can be deceiving? Mr Harrison glared at us. "I think you've outstayed your welcome," he said.

I hadn't actually been aware of much of a welcome but said nothing. We headed for the door.

"What?" said Geraint. "No thanks for helping with this *terrible* crime? No praise for effort—" but the door was closed on his expression of confused innocence.

"What was all that about?" asked Angela as we reached the top of their drive and crossed back over to ours.

Geraint said, "Well, my maths isn't very good but whatever is half of 20,000 pounds, I reckon is what that was all about."

Angela didn't look much enlightened.

"They would have had to call the police to get a crime number for the insurance, when the dog was pinched." This was Geraint's world's territory so he explained it, "This is a smart area so they would have attended quite quickly – it looks like it was Plum who showed up. He'd have probably had a look around, he'd have spotted the dodgy window straight away and realised why they were pretending it had been the front door – to get the insurance. Then they must have had a little chat and agreed a price for him to keep quiet, a nice little backhander for them all, until you rocked up as eye-witnesses and nearly blew it!"

"Then why arrest Jimmy?"

"Well the police probably thought it *was* a Traveller, that's the way police minds work. Plus, it looks as if he is doing a good job; he got an arrest so looks good on his record, and it shows the insurance company it *is* a real crime for sure, why *not* arrest Jimmy? He might have been the thief! Then you and Simon rock up again and blow *that* out of the water. It got Jimmy out but also nearly blew the insurance scam as well, which is more important, to them anyway!"

"So they don't care about the dog?"

"I doubt it. And they certainly don't care that there's an innocent man in prison either."

Angela looked sad that there was so much wickedness in the world.

We arrived home.

"Your editor would never have published that story, showing the police up," said Angela as an afterthought. "You told me he needs to keep well in with the police."

"Of course not, but our copper couldn't count on that, and still can't."

Angela took his arm. He seemed to have recovered a lot of the ground he had lost over the story about the meeting, I noticed.

There was an envelope on the front doormat when we got back. It was to me from Frank. It was a card and a short note paper-clipped to a flyer advertising short cruises. The note just said, 'Fancy another one of these?"

I had to smile. I felt relief like a warm breeze. Frank and I had had affairs and breakups before, though none so serious as these last and the way we healed afterwards was always with a short cruise: being quite wealthy has its advantages. We found cruises restful and reassuring – a guarantee of our continued togetherness if only because neither of us could swim. It was time to go home. Again. Or maybe not? Maybe living together was not such a great idea? Maybe just seeing each other, not too much, not too much togetherness, would work better? I pocketed the card and poured a glass of wine. I wouldn't answer too quickly.

Chapter Thirteen
More Visitors

Geraint stayed for half a glass of wine and to make a late dinner date with Angela as they had not had time to eat much of their brunch at the cafe. It had been quite a day. The late edition had reported the murder with a banner headline, as not a lot happens in our town, with lots of hints at salacious details and possible facts which the paper didn't know but which they could imply and invite their readers to salivate over. There was also a photograph of Jake captioned as 'gardener arrested' and, for some unexplained reason, quite a bit about Jake's Jamaican origins.

It had not been Geraint's name on the report, which Angie was pleased about. He had kept his word and not abused her friendship even though it would have cost him the 'scoop'. I was impressed too. The fact that Jake had now been released and could never have been guilty because the story that had led to his being arrested had been a tiny little lie meant to appease a racist would, of course, have to wait until a later edition – probably Monday's – as this one had gone to press before Angela had told the police her little secret and blown the case.

Angela was flustered about what to wear on her date.

"I haven't felt like this since … er …?" she stammered excitedly, unable to finish the sentence.

"Since you were a teenager?" I suggested.

"No, I never felt like this as a teenager. Or as an adult!"

"Didn't you misbehave in your teens, do wild things?"

"Heck, no! I'd have been thrown out. I've been short-changed by Life, I'm going to make up for it now. I'm going to do 'wild things' like they've never been done before."

She said this with such vigour and fervour I began to have actual fears for Geraint's wellbeing.

Angela looked thoughtful then said, "My mother always warned me against being 'a floozy' – well I've tried being respectable and, quite frankly, they can stuff it! I'm going to give 'floozy' a try – must be better than being a docile doormat!" I was rather lost for words.

Angela went to get ready for her date and I prepared a 'fridge banquet' – pooling all the leftovers into a kind of mad buffet – cold or reheated on a plate in front of the telly for myself. I was just settling into a Saturday night binge-watching my boxset of *Cheers* and admiring the gorgeous Sam when the doorbell rang.

The plain-clothed policeman was at our door saying there'd been 'a development'. Angela came downstairs dressed almost smartly and almost ready to go out. We clarified that this evening call was about the murder, not the dog theft, as things were getting a bit blurred. He said it was about the murder (which made sense really, this being a Saturday night and police officers entitled to time off as much as the rest of us when less urgent matters hung in the balance). He came in, wiped his feet, declined a coffee, and asked could we explain about mysterious comings and goings from our house in the night by a person believed to be male, ethnic origin uncertain but often dressed in work-clothes as might befit someone like a gardener. The sightings had been reported to them whilst they had been making routine enquiries around the close looking for any sightings of suspicious people. This was asked with another hard stare at Angela who floundered and looked to me.

"That would be my lover," I explained. "He wears such clothes though he's not a gardener, only sometimes. Ex-lover actually. He hasn't been here for a while. Parting of the ways and all that."

The policeman's eyes stopped peering at Angela and slowly swivelled over to look at me.

"I see," he said after quite a while, "and can you vouch for your, er, friend's whereabouts on the night in question?"

"He would have been at work I expect. He's been night-cleaning at Feltham's for a while now. We have been meeting during the day. Before we broke up, I mean. Or with his new girlfriend come to think of it – not sure when that got started."

The copper looked suddenly quite sad, as if a policeman's salary was suddenly not enough to compensate for the sort of lifestyle he obviously wasn't having compared to some others who had women to visit both in the night and in the afternoon.

"And what does he look like, your … er … friend?"

I held up a hand, "About yay tall, grey eyes, light brown hair so no … not black. Not whom Mrs Fitzsimmons was talking to on Wednesday."

"Well," said our officer, reading from his notes, "there's been a development there too: I had misunderstood Mr Fitzsimmons – his wife had only been talking to the stranger *at a distance*, from an upstairs window. The man was standing in their front

garden. It was a bright sunny day. He was wearing a
hat so his face was in shadow. He wore long sleeves
and gardening gloves so Mrs Fitzsimmons just
assumed it was Jake but didn't actually see his face very
clearly. She *thought* he was black as he had a slight
accent which she couldn't place so … so we're
following other enquiries. Some people in the close
mentioned strange night-time visitations at this house
for example. Did your, er … friend know Mrs
Fitzsimmons?"

"No, and he hasn't been here for weeks – we're
through."

I'd probably never think of Simon as an ex-lover
ever again but as an ex- 'er …friend'.

"I'll need to question him – we need to follow all
leads."

I wrote Simon's contact details on a piece of
paper. I hoped and trusted he would have a decent
alibi for the night in question. I trusted he would,
either through working a night-shift or through not
sleeping alone in his newly vacated parental home
with his new love.

"Have you let Jake go yet?" asked Angela.

"Yes, there was nothing to link him with the case
now your neighbour has explained more clearly what
his wife told him and the truth about what you told
him has come out. Pity you told him that lie, wasted

police time but we won't be pursuing that. Easy mistake to make. Thank you for explaining about the night visitor. I'll get in touch. Um ... you witnessed that dog-napping as well, didn't you?" he asked, hesitating by the door.

"Yes," I said.

"You seem to lead complicated lives," he commented.

He left.

It was terrifying to think that Simon might now be a suspect.

"Are they going to arrest everybody who's ever visited the close?" I asked. "What about the milkie and the postie? What about Martin, he was here for five minutes ... oh my god! What *about* Martin – remember what she said to him when he was here? Did he come back to do her in? Or was it the milkie. he *said* he *found* the body on the path in the garden but did he *put* it there?"

"Don't be silly," said Angela. "You'll give yourself nightmares, or you'll be thinking I did it next. I was asleep in my room at the time of the murder but you've only got my word for that."

"Why would you murder Edith?" I asked, shocked.

She ignored me but in a very sarcastic sort of way and rolled her eyes.

"Why would the milkie? Because she hadn't rinsed out his bottles?"

"Is that a euphemism for something?"

More eye rolling.

"I'll ring Simon anyway and warn him," I said, my dignity ruffled.

I got on with that. Simon answered and appreciated my calling him. He thought for a minute and remembered he'd been doing a night-watch shift at a site with another guy on the night in question so that was no problem. I gave him an update about our visit to the Harrisons and that Jimmy would be released very soon and we ended the call on a friendly note.

Geraint arrived then in his evening finery, which looked remarkably similar to his afternoon finery but he had made something of an effort and Angela, halfway to glamour and with one eyelash mascaraed and the other not, left with him. I doubt either of them would notice anything amiss with the appearance of the other as wide-eyed as they were.

As they left I looked up my own digital window on a better world and settled down to watch it.

I had just pressed the button to the DVD to commence when the doorbell rang. Cursing slightly I paused it.

Expecting Angela to have forgotten her keys or

something, I answered it, but it was Mr Fitzsimmons standing on the doorstep, looking woebegone in a grey cardigan. I knew his house was now a crime scene, with everything locked up to avoid 'interference with evidence' and suchlike so he had had to book in at a hotel for the time-being, somewhere in town and hand over his house-keys to the police. I felt sorry for him. On top of everything else he was suffering he was effectively homeless.

"Do you mind if I come in?" he asked. "I just need someone to talk to," he said.

My heart went out to him and I asked him in. He obviously needed some company in the midst of all the trauma. I poured us both a drink.

"I hope I'm not interrupting anything?" he asked, sitting on the sofa I'd indicated, his shoulders slumped. "I can't go in the house yet – not sure if I could actually, it all reminds me of her, of Edith, and what I've lost."

His hand went up to his forehead and he struggled to control himself.

"I am sorry. I think I'm still in shock. That terrible day … she was all I had. Who could have done such a thing? She wouldn't hurt a fly, she was so caring, so helpful … always wanting to look after others. She looked after me, you remember, even the last thing she said to me was to make sure I had remembered the dratted sandwiches she had made for my journey. I answered her a bit crossly, do you remember? That is haunting me – my last words and I was irritated by her fussing over me! I was in a rush, I didn't even get to …" He sobbed and the next words were croaked and he pulled out a hanky, " … say goodbye properly, or kiss her goodbye. I was so keen to get to that blasted party and not miss the train." His voice was choked into heartrending sobs.

I sat on the chair next to the sofa. I felt I ought to put an arm around him or something but didn't like to; I wished Angela was there, she was much better at this sort of thing than I am. He seemed to pull himself together a little. "You do remember, don't you?" he asked, querulously. I said that of course I did and that she had obviously loved him very much which, unfortunately, set him off again into his handkerchief. My tandoori was going cold. I stood up to put it in the fridge for later and offered him a drink which he accepted.

"I'm sorry we never got to know you and Angela better. We kept ourselves to ourselves. We didn't know Martin and Angela very well either come to that. I wish you'd known Edith better, she was such a lovely person. I loved her so much and now she's gone."

As the drink didn't seem to be helping any, I didn't offer him another one but he went on … "At least we had that last day together doing our beautiful garden.

It was our joy and our best hobby, so lovely to have someone you can share the little things in life with, don't you think? Is it like that with you and Angela?"

A bit taken aback I assured him we were 'just friends' but that, yes, I did appreciate close relationships and sharing.

He smiled weakly, "Sorry, I was just assuming. … with Martin the way he is and everything."

The doorbell rang. I wasn't used to this hectic lifestyle.

On the doorstep this time were two people I didn't recognise: a man and a woman of advanced years who both smiled up at me through spectacles.

"Angela?" said the woman, who was bent almost double over her walking frame which balanced precariously on the narrow front step. Her male companion held her arm in support. "We are Mr and Mrs Brown, we live further up the close at number 48. I'm Elisha, this is Henry."

I explained who I was and that Angela was out for the evening and invited them in. They stepped slowly across the threshold, walking was obviously painful for her and not easy for him. I guessed they were at least in their eighties. When we got to the living room, Mr Fitzsimons had stood up and was preparing to leave, thanking me for my hospitality but that he had to be going. He and the two newcomers nodded at each other and I got the impression they knew each other but that neither party were in raptures about that.

"We are sorry for your loss," said Henry Brown, a bit stiffly, I thought.

"It must have been a terrible shock," said Elisha, in a formal sort of way.

Mr Fitzsimmons nodded in reply and took his leave, closing the front door behind him.

"We won't sit down," said Elisha, more cheerfully, "might not be able to get up again." She pointed at Henry, "Rheumatoid arthritis," and at herself, "Osteoparosis and a few other bits and pieces. Not as much fun as you'd expect. We just came to bring these."

She proffered a sheet of paper. I could see a list of names and addresses on it with email addresses and phone numbers – I had completely forgotten about the petition. The blank copies which Angela and I had brought home, intending to collect names, lay languishing, still blank, in some drawer somewhere. Judging by the speed at which my two visitors could walk it must have taken them the whole of the past two days to visit all the houses represented there. All the addresses were of the close, I noticed, but none of them were of the numbers near our own house.

"We asked the people we knew – there were some we knew well enough not to ask," said Henry. "Most people signed. Did you like our flowers?"

I must have looked a bit blank then, "Oh in the blue pot? By the door?"

They smiled and nodded, pleased at my recollection. I knew the little pot of flowers was still on the windowsill, wilting fast, and I had thought it a romantic gesture by a certain reporter as had, I'd guessed, Angela, though neither of us had said so, but apparently it was from these two.

Elisha smiled and took up the story, "I wanted to say thank you. We asked our son to drop them off on his way back after bringing us home from that awful meeting I thought Angela was so brave speaking up like that."

"Well that was very nice of you," I said, although it seemed a bit excessive.

Elisha smiled. "You see, I know about meetings like that. I'm Jewish. My mother escaped on the kindertransport train, one of the last trains before they closed the borders. Closing borders always kills people. She was a young child, she never saw any of her family again. So you see, I know a bit about racism and where it can lead, how it starts, and it starts with meetings like that – when nobody says anything and people get scapegoated and blamed for things they have not done. Nobody saying anything is what lets the fascists win, but Angela did say something. I was too scared – we both were – we saw who was there, in their green uniforms and badges."

She stopped, a bit breathless. Henry hooked his arm through hers and took her hand in his. She smiled at him.

Henry said, "Any kind of racism, whether it's attacking Jews or Muslims or Travellers … it's all the same – poison."

Elisha nodded, "It was difficult for us when we moved to the close. Henry isn't Jewish but when I mentioned that I am to neighbours at coffee mornings, the invitations stopped coming and our children were not invited to play – not by everybody, just by some. The Fitzsimmons' walked out of our first 'welcome to our new home' garden party as soon as they knew my little secret. They didn't say anything but they didn't have to. It's better now up our end of the close, we got to know each other and it got better. But some even objected to that nice man who was a gardener – so stupid. Any kind of racism is wrong, that's why the Zionists have got it wrong," she said. "Can you get these signatures to that young woman – put them together with yours? They're handing them into the council on the 30th."

I took the list of names, didn't mention we had collected none to add to them, and offered them a drink but they said they were only 'popping in' but maybe next time and maybe we could visit and we could chat more. They turned to go, Elisha manoeuvring her walking frame around the furniture.

"Poor Mr Fitzsimmons," I said by way of conversation on our slow way back to the door.

"Are you friends?" Elisha asked, stopping to look at me.

"No, this is only the second time we've spoken," I said. "He's very upset, obviously."

Elisha looked at me quite intently. "You be careful around him, my dear. When you are old, like us, people often don't see you and they think you're deaf and they say things they might not say if they think they might be heard by anybody else."

I was interested.

"At the bus stop by the common," she said, stopping to lean on her frame and get her breath, "waiting to go into town — until last year I was quite mobile, couldn't drive anymore but I could still go for short walks and use the buses. They pulled up in that big car of theirs, she got out, he was driving. They were laying into each other, verbally I mean, really loud. Nobody was hitting but he was saying dreadful things to her, really dreadful. She was shouting back but in tears. She walked off back towards the house and he sped off. He took no notice of me. I was so shocked — it was so nasty. We have our rows," she smiled at Henry who smiled back and I saw a hand squeeze pass between them, "but not like that. Vicious. And she looked scared. That's the difference, someone being scared, and I've seen her a few times walking up past our house to the path at the top in tears. Once I asked her if she'd like to come in and have a cup of tea. She was so distressed but she looked so shocked, as if she hadn't seen me there, and didn't even reply. She just glared at me and walked on. I didn't ask again after that. Now I wish I had." Elisha looked sad at the memory and the thought of what she could have done.

"She wouldn't have spoken to you, my love," said Henry. "You know what she was like. She never came to our little get-togethers once she knew. And, as well as that, he was probably well in control of her, you know what domestic abuse does to people. It silences them so they can't seek help. And she called at people's houses to tell them not to give work to that nice black gardener. She didn't come to our house to do that," he smiled at me, "I feel quite proud of that – she knew she'd get short shrift! And we didn't bother to call to ask her to sign the petition either. It's very sad that some people who are being oppressed themselves don't fight it but pass it on by oppressing others, very sad ... but true."

"Mind you, that was just as well," said Elisha. "We were calling at people's houses last night and if we had called at hers we might have run into the murderer! She wouldn't have supported Travellers anyway, for sure. She turned them away when they would call. I buy lucky white heather or clothes pegs or give over some washing to be done by hand, or have my palm read of a morning."

Henry rolled his eyes in mockery at this but she wasn't accepting that, "Get out of here! People spend a *fortune* on counselling, a chance to chew over problems with a kind stranger. It's worth every penny and is a good service! Imagine what it was like in the old villages, everyone knowing your business, no-one to tell your secrets to, then the Gypsies come along. They'd listen and not tell. They give some kind advice and take your secrets away with them when they left!"

"Oh yeah?" said Henry, only half joking. "What secrets did you tell them? Anything for me to worry about?" Elisha laughed too and elbowed him, nearly tipping over with her frame.

They laughed and she gave him a kiss. "There's another reason the Zionists have got it wrong," she said, "Henry isn't Jewish and we get along quite well!"

"Early days yet, dear," he said. "We've only been together sixty years!"

"What the Fitzsimmons don't know is, there is a Travellers' sign on their gate – left there to warn others. 'Don't call here'. It looks like just a few lines, means nothing to anyone else but roughly translates as 'mean and nasties live here'!" said Elisha with a chuckle before checking herself. "Oh, mustn't speak ill of the dead."

"Is there anything on our gate?" I asked. Elisha said she hadn't noticed but I wondered if she was being diplomatic.

"Do you speak Travellers' language then?"

"Shelta and Romani? No, I know a few of the signs is all. One of the women who called, we would chat and got quite friendly and she told me about it. I have respect for them. They died in the same camps where we died. I feel a camaraderie with them. My mother told me about all that."

We were quiet for a moment and thought about 'all that'.

"Just as well you didn't call at their house yesterday morning either. You might have been the ones to find the body and might have been accused of murder. What a horrible thought," I said.

"I don't think so, dear," said Elisha. "I can scuff ankles with this thing but between us Henry and I haven't the strength to harm a piece of paper. Who did find her?"

"The milkman."

"Poor guy! Not Mr Fitzsimmons then?"

"No, he was away on an overnight beano with the golf club crowd."

Elisha looked at me again. "You just be careful, dear. I don't trust that man – not one inch!"

We eventually got to the door. They stepped slowly off the step and walked sedately down the drive. They waved as they turned to go slowly back up the close. The whole trip to our house must have taken a good hour I reckoned, thinking how we take youth and health for granted – which got me back to thinking about Simon once more so I went back to *Cheers* again and the lovely Sam.

Angela got back later. I was asleep on the sofa. I hadn't intended to stay up as if I was a controlling parent of a wayward teenager but had just dozed off. She and Geraint did that thing on the front doorstep of awkwardly ending a first date. I resisted the urge to peek from the curtains like an anxious mother to see if they kissed or not. Whether they did or not, Angela was bright-eyed enough to warn me that this was not the last date she and Geraint would be sharing so I'd better get used to it.

Geraint and Angela had called at the Gypsy site on the way back to find out the latest to see if words had been kept and, sure enough, Jimmy had been released. Da had ridden down into town to collect his son from outside the station, as police don't provide transport for the wrongfully arrested, and brought him home in fine style, riding bareback on the larger of the skewbalds. A banquet had been had of sorts to welcome him home with actual meat, courtesy of the local pigeon population, and a cake baked on the open fire in the cast-iron pot – Pearl's speciality.

It had been a bit late to invite Angela and myself but could we call there sometime and have a cuppa and be thanked? They would be moving on soon, now our witness statements had been taken, Billy and Liam's names were cleared and the assault case dropped. The forensics were probably still looking at the blood which had splashed from the broken nose onto his shirt but even if there was any nazi blood on his shirt, or on Liam's jersey, our testimony would show neither of them had been the aggressor. The dog-napping remained a mystery but thanks to Simon's deft work with his camera, it was clearly not Jimmy who had carried it out. The police would have to pay more attention to my evidence and take it seriously if the mysterious Anthea didn't ring and tell all – as we hoped she would – which could then lead the police to the actual gang leaders not just the 'gophers.'

Chapter Fourteen

More Changes

The paper reported that, in the murder case, the recently accused had been released and that police were now pursuing other lines of enquiry. This report was on page three or four so had to be sought out. It was obviously not as saleable as the great news of a murder and arrest. Far more people would have seen and would remember Jake's black face under the headline about a murder than would ever read the retraction. The news of Jimmy's release was also a small paragraph at the bottom of page two which you really had to hunt for to find but the front-page story that had reported the young Traveller arrested for theft would surely live on in the collective memory.

The next day we did our surreptitious early Sunday morning fortnightly shop at the unfashionable end of the supermarket spectrum to refill the freezer and cupboards. Early morning was the best time to avoid unwanted observation and comment, although our cares about the world's approval had receded to such an extent that we had actually abandoned the under-the-cover-of-midnight ventures into the world of retail and were quite blasé about unloading the car on the front drive in broad daylight with no regard for the consequences of our neighbours spotting the bags and the brands, like the couple of reckless, thick-skinned devil-may- care rebels we had become. Then we headed over to the common with some chocolates to take up their invitation and share in some of the joy of Jimmy's return home. I knew this might mean an encounter with Simon in his new life but was able to assure Angela that I was fine about how things had turned out.

As we arrived at the site we were greeted as old friends by Pearl who left the fireside where she and Siobhan were teaching a group of youngsters the art of cooking on an open fire. "How are you?" she asked. "How can I ever thank you?"

I just smiled but Angela hesitated and then said, "Well actually, I was wondering …?"

Pearl looked pleased and surprised, "Name it," she said, jokingly, her arms outspread to include all the largesse of the site,. "What? Free pegs? Some cake? Firewood? Some washing?"

Angela said, "I wonder if we can have a chat?"

"Sure," said Pearl, realising this was serious, and Angela took her arm. "You can come too," Angela said to me. "This concerns you too." We all walked together over to where some folding chairs had been left in the shade of a tree which was just coming into blossom.

"Someone said you might be able to help me," said Angela.

"If I can," said Pearl. "Give me your hand."

Angela did, and immediately, as it does when someone holds our hand in a friendly way, there was a link of intimacy between them.

"Now," said Pearl, kindly, "what is it that's troubling you?" She was looking at the lines in Angela's palm but I got the impression that it was the listening that was the important part of this.

And Angie told her. She told her all about the decades of a lost marriage; the years of loneliness; the husband leaving her and why; the finding out about his affair and the years of lying, the whole lifetime of lying; how she felt she could never trust anyone again or let anyone close to her, although there was someone now she felt she *could* like – a lot – and feelings she had not had before or for a long time. How she felt so angry at what her husband had done and angry at herself for being so deceived and all the

234

wasted years and that she couldn't find a way forward.

Pearl listened and nodded and held her hand as she spoke. It was the first time Angela had said most of this though she had told me bits and hinted at the rest. I had thought she was working through it and putting it behind her and that time would heal but maybe sometimes Time needs a little help to get things moving.

"The lying is the worst. That's hurt me so badly, it makes me so angry! How could he do that to me?"

Pearl thought for a while.

"Firstly," she said, quite gently, "those years were not wasted because they brought you here – to where you are today, to where you need to go next – with all you've learned from those years. They have passed but they have not been wasted, and secondly … was it you he was lying to, or was it himself? Was it you, or was it the whole world? Did he set out to lie, or did he just not know the truth? When did the lying start, I ask you?"

We were all quiet for a moment.

Pearl said, "Nobody tells the truth when it isn't safe to tell the truth. Was he safe?"

Angela was thinking. I was thinking of what she had said about his father, 'always banging on about 'pouffes' and 'queers' and how dangerous they were and his mother not much better.

At what point had the young Martin hid himself away and run from who it was that nature intended him to be? It hadn't been Angela he had been lying to – it *was* the whole world, a world which told him he could never tell the truth or be true to himself *and* be safe, a world which insisted he lie forever.

Angela's face had gone all creased. She shook her head then nodded. She whispered in a hoarse voice, "He wasn't safe … ever. When I met him he was already locked in a lie. It wasn't me. I didn't make this happen … nor did he." Pearl handed her a corner of one of her shawls to wipe her eyes and I dug out a handkerchief too.

"He hurt you very badly," she said, as Angela wept and nodded. "And it'll take a while to recover but you will recover and it was never aimed at you I think. I'm sure he loved you, just not that way – the man and woman way. It sounds like he has started to find out how to be happy by being true to himself, but now you have to be brave too and find a way to be happy. You can stop living a lie too. There are a lot of ways to be happy, you just have to find one that's right for you. The lying can stop now."

Angela had a bit of a cry and Pearl held her while she did. We were still sat under the tree on a Sunday morning in Spring but it felt as if something had shifted.

"Is that helpful?" asked Pearl. Angie nodded and said thank you and smiled through her tears and hanky. "Do I cross your palm with silver or something?" she asked.

"Not today, you can have that one for free," laughed Pearl, squeezing Angela's hand then letting go.

Angela smiled.

"Well that's a start," said Pearl, "come and talk any time you like. Life is difficult and we all need to help each other if we can. Do you want to talk some more now?"

Angela shook her head. "That has helped actually, I didn't think of it that way before. Thank you."

It felt like our little chat had ended. Angela was drying her eyes and sniffing.

"Talking helps sometimes. Makes sense of things. Take me: I was one of the children taken from our parents because they were gypsies – it was policy then – in the '60s- told me my parents were dead. It took me years to find my way back. But I did. And I realised it wasn't the social workers' fault – they were only doing what they were told. And you learn stuff from trauma – how to cope. Makes you stronger – able to help others."

"I don't think I want to be any stronger, or learn anymore," said Angela, "My brain's full."

"Come on then," said Pearl and she led us back towards the fire. She took us to meet Jimmy who, along with Billy and the other young men, was busy again among a fresh crop of cars in need of repair which were parked on the grass.

Jimmy was as awkward and shy as any young man of his age, as Hugo had been, and with the requisite attempts at facial hair-growth commensurate with that age group. To help our visit along, Pearl suggested he show us around the camp. He took up the suggestion and we headed off with him while Pearl went back to her culinary class. Billy nodded at us in a friendly way, as did Liam, from under various raised hoods and bonnets. I felt a pang of guilt knowing that soon I would be the instrument of destroying Billy's clever cover of 'affable honest guy' and expose him as thief and organiser of thieves and break his parents' hearts. He thanked us for reporting to the police what we had seen and getting the assault charges dropped. Fern had told them all about Simon and his photographs of the door that proved Jimmy's innocence. He said not to leave before allowing him to give us a 'bottle of something special' he had bought as a thank you.

Of course we wanted to see the old, Victorian trailer with its tiny, carved interior. It was surely far too small for anyone to live within, we commented. Jimmy explained, with some pride, how Travellers live outdoors with trailers just providing some shelter but mostly storage and carriage space, which was why living in a house felt like being in a trap for most Travellers and staying in the same place all the time was most unnatural.

Jimmy introduced us to the horses and we watched a harness being made but declined the offer of a bareback ride around the common. A loud intermittent crashing noise which I had noticed before was explained when we went around behind the main trailers and found two men, Matthew and another, with sledge hammers standing in the middle of a heap of white metal and smashing it up with the hammers. The heap was the remnants, apparently, of washing machines and a dishwasher. The men stopped at our approach. Both were wearing tee-shirts which were covered in sweat on this cool Spring day. We must have looked mystified, and maybe a little scared, so Jimmy said how the items could be broken up, the electrical parts salvaged and the metal sold or recycled to bring in some much-needed cash. But it was very hard work breaking up the metal items with hammers.

"We've been recycling long before it was called 'recycling'," he said, with a smile. "They say gypsies are dirty and messy but the only mess we make is trying to clear up after you lot!" He was looking at us. I recalled how many washing machines had broken down just in my own kitchen and been thrown out.

Matthew wagged his finger at Jimmy, his eyes full of humour, "Yeh, and this is *real* recycling, not that wussy stuff you and Billy-boy get up to." Jimmy grinned a bit sheepishly.

He had a bit more banter that I couldn't follow with the two men and then we left.

It looked hard work and the hammering continued as we moved away.

I couldn't help thinking how nice it must be to have people around you all the time. I looked over at Pearl surrounded by her grandchildren and others and Da with his sons and sons' friends and cousins. There was no loneliness here. It was like a small, mobile village where everybody knew everybody else and everyone chipped in with keeping the whole thing going. The children seemed to be looked after by everybody and the work shared out among all present. No paid babysitters here and no-one left out of the campfire meals, although I expected they were often sparse.

We saw Fern and her sister, Siobhan, sitting near Pearl making wooden pegs from sticks out of a pile that looked as if it might have been collected on the common. As we watched two children brought another bundle to add to the pile. Some were sorted for peg-work, others for firewood or kindling. The adults were using knives to whittle the wood. I remembered newspaper reports of knives being found at gypsy sites with horrific implications of their use – none of the reports had ever said anything about peg-whittling or firewood. Younger children were working next to them, sandpapering the end results into useful items for laundry-day. Pearl got up to fetch us each a cup of tea and a griddle cake. She introduced us to Megan – Billy's wife – who smiled up at us from where she was encouraging a small child to take a few steps.

I was just about to ask Jimmy what Matthew had meant by the 'wussy stuff' Billy-boy had 'been doing', when we saw a police car approaching in all its white and orange regalia. People moved away from what they were doing and towards the car as it pulled up. They looked wary and watchful but also hopeful. Three uniformed officers got out – all men – and two began heaving full, black bin-bags out of the back of the car onto the grass. The third handed a pink form on a clipboard to Da, who had gone up to the car, and handed him a pen to sign it.

The clothes had been discovered not to be stolen after all and were being returned. But there was more. One of the policemen asked to speak to 'William Lewis' and Billy walked over. I heard Jimmy mutter, "I wish they'd quit calling him 'William', his name's Billy!"

We all expected him to also need to sign

something to acknowledge the dropping of charges or whatever but instead the other two officers stepped forward quite suddenly, grabbed him, twisted him around, and I saw handcuffs being forced onto his hands. It all happened so quickly he was caught quite unawares. One officer had him in an arm-lock and pushed him towards the car where the door was being held open. He twisted away, struggling, to stop himself being thrust into the car, shouting, "No! What are you doing!?" They had both pushed him towards the car before the rest of us knew what was happening while the other said, quite loudly, "William Lewis, you are under arrest on suspicion of murder—"

Da ran forward and was remonstrating with the policeman who spoke back to him forcefully but we couldn't hear what was said.

Billy was shouting, "I didn't – I didn't … you're all mad!" He looked over towards his father and yelled, "Tell Megan I didn't do this, Da! Tell her I—"

"She knows already, son!" shouted Da back to him, "We all do."

But then Billy was pushed into the car, the policemen got in either side of him, the car door was slammed and the driver leapt back into his seat. I realised the engine had not been switched off. The car backed off up the track very quickly, the rest of the policeman's statement of rights was lost to the car's interior. Da shouted and took off up the track after the car which spun round on its own axis and roared away. Billy's younger brother and cousins ran after it, children ran out of its way, a child shouted "Daddy!", Megan had stood up, staring, the small child taken up into her arms as she stared at the car in disbelief. Pearl took a step, her face drawn in shock and horror, then I saw, as if a ton weight had suddenly fallen down on her shoulders, her knees gave way from under her and she collapsed on the ground.

Others ran to help her. I watched in horror. I tried to imagine how it would hit me if my son had been arrested for murder and pushed the thought away as unbearable. I was dumbstruck. All my suspicions about Billy had now been confirmed but this was much worse than anything I had suspected. I could see it in my mind's eye: Billy returning to our close that night, looking for another rich picking. The dog-napping had failed or nearly failed but here was another house. Maybe he had noticed the car was not in the drive and the houselights not on and thought the house empty but then he had run into Mrs Edith Fitzsimmons as she walked in her garden and, to stop her identifying him as the thief, hit her with the first thing to hand – her own hedge-trimmer. Merciless. Left her there to be found by the milkman in the morning and made his getaway, back to the common to sleep and then back into the campsite the next day, cool as a cucumber and taking the chance to go to Buttersville with us to be out of the way for a while and cover his track.

Jimmy was free but for how long and how many of these Travellers, who, like Billy, presented as friendly and innocent, were involved in the organised gang which the mysterious Anthea might well now tell me about if only to save her own skin? Da was relaying to the group what the policeman had said. They had seen blood on one of the shirts they had confiscated when acting on suspicion of the clothes at the site being stolen property and sent it to forensics.

"Some of the spots were the nazi's blood—" said Da.

"It weren't spots, Da," interrupted Liam, "Billy broke the fecker's nose. There was a torrent of it – there was a whole splash on his sleeve—"

Pearl, who was sitting up now, took one hand away from her face to slap his leg automatically and say half-heartedly, "Language!"

"Sorry Auntie Pearl," muttered Liam. "But he *did* break his nose," he ended, with some pride in his voice. "That's why he got blood on him but none on me," said Liam. He then turned away, looking miserable with guilt that his cousin was arrested and he was not.

"Anyway, the police scientists matched the

bloodstains on Billy's shirtsleeve with the nazi's but then some other spots showed up on the back of the shoulder of it ... and *that* matched with the lady who was killed," finished Da.

"No way did Billy do that!" was the general outcry. I wondered if it was being said for our benefit. I wondered if they all knew about Billy's night-time activities, only this time he had encountered a witness and acted in haste.

"My son is no killer," cried Da.

"Why is the blood on his back? Is he supposed to have killed her when she was standing behind him?" Liam wanted to know. "How is he supposed to have done that, with a boomerang?"

Others speculated that the police had put the blood there to frame him.

I felt the police would no doubt sort out these minor details in good time and Anthea's story would, no doubt, flesh out the whole horrible story. Our little cul-de-sac had twice been hit by the same gang in the same week and the second time it had been murder.

It felt too painful to be part of what was happening, so we decided to leave.

We went to say our farewells to Jimmy who was standing by Liam and Da in deep discussion. We didn't feel we ought to intrude but felt it rude to just leave when the family were in such distress. As we approached a phone pinged. Da had it in his pocket and took the call but then handed it to Liam who turned away to take the call. We heard him say, "Yes? No, he can't do that tomorrow – I can though and maybe his brother." He looked over to Jimmy and said, "Shift on the vans tomorrow, you up for it?" Jimmy nodded glumly and Liam continued, saying, "Yes, two of us can … okay … afternoon shift … yeh that's fine," and ended the call.

I couldn't help saying, "You're going to go to work?"

I thought that with Billy arrested, this wasn't the time.

"We still gotta eat," said Liam. "Of course I don't want to but kids being hungry won't help Billy," he nodded at Jimmy. "Half a day's work tomorrow, whoever's free."

Jimmy nodded.

We had begun to mutter our goodbyes. I felt a hypocrite saying how sorry I was at the present problem and that we could do nothing to help this time, knowing as I did that Billy was not the innocent he pretended to be but they did all seem genuinely shocked, as indeed I was, that he had gone as far as murder.

"You helped get Jimmy out – that'll do for now. This one's more serious. No way did Billy harm that woman in any way but we'll have our work cut out proving it. He slept up on the common that night with no-one to witness but his cousin and he was asleep too of course," said Da, looking distressed and worried as we took our leave.

They turned back to discussing the situation and we left.

Chapter Fifteen
Hard Facts

On the way back I told Angela my theory: how Billy, and probably his brother, cousin, and others, were all in prime positions to 'case the joint' wherever they went to spot chances for theft and then carry them out either themselves or with associates, like our friends in Buttersville. I explained how our wild goose-chase there had been just a ruse to cover their tracks, to stop us going to the police once we knew about the blue-and white car and to trick us into thinking they were innocent *and* give the real thieves, their friends Anthea and Leon, a chance to hide the dog if they hadn't already sold it – or even kill it. Also, the blood on Billy's shirt must have happened after he came across Mrs F while snooping around her garden that night, looking to rob the house – he hadn't expected to find her there so had killed her to silence her.

"When?" said Angela. "He was sat in front of us at the meeting by 7 p.m. – she was alive at 6.15 because that was when her husband was leaving."

"In the night, he was supposed to be sleeping on the common, avoiding the police, and within shouting distance if the skinheads had showed up but we don't *know* he was there. His cousin was asleep or he might have been in on it, they work as a team. It doesn't take long to kill someone, it's not far from the common – he might even have seen the drive was empty and assumed the house to be empty. I'm sure he was involved in the dog stealing even though it was his brother who got arrested. He works all over town, lots of opportunities, he could easily have come down in the night … we don't know exactly what time she was killed."

"Why would Edith have been gardening in the middle of the night!"

"I don't know, maybe she was looking at the moon, maybe she was ringing her husband and can only get a signal in the garden at their house. I don't know the details! Maybe she likes walking in the garden at night, maybe she was feeding a hedgehog, like you do. We'd have to ask her husband that. We don't know but Billy was obviously the killer … I've got a feeling!"

"Right, a feeling – better lock him up then!" she said.

"It's her blood on his shirt," I pointed out. "How else could it have got there? He's guilty of her murder, we know that much, but it's just I think he's guilty of more besides. They all are. Look how they're quite happy to carry on going to work, like nothing's happened – quite callous, like hardened criminals. They probably knew he'd be caught one day and he was in her garden because of the stuff he normally does – looking for chances to steal. You heard Liam, they have no income unless they find work or can sell stuff. Don't you see? It all fits!"

"But they found the blue-and-white car," she said. "We wouldn't have done that without them! Why would they have done that if they were all in on it!"

"To make them look innocent, of course," I said, exasperated, and feeling a sympathy with Sherlock Holmes dealing with a particularly obtuse Watson. "AND to get us to go to Buttersville to warn the other two and it stopped us going to the police. Don't you see? They're very clever."

By the look on her face she didn't see much at all and was going a bit tight-lipped on me as we pulled into the drive and let ourselves in. Over the low wall we could see the black-and-yellow tape on the garden gate and door, shining in the afternoon sun and still defining the house next door as a crime scene. The close was busy with cars as people returned from church.

We had put a good dinner in the slow cooker before we had left in the morning and it was probably ready now, although the company didn't promise to be good. Angela liked Billy. I suspected it was because he had called her gorgeous and she had liked all his and Liam's stories on the way to Buttersville and had enjoyed telling them about films she'd seen. And she liked Pearl too, I suppose we both did but we had to face facts and not be taken in by superficial impressions and people's charm.

"That poor man," I said, nodding towards the Fitzsimmons' house, to change the subject and find some common ground.

"Terrible," she agreed. "How do you cope with something like that?"

I opened the door and the scent of a well-cooked stew greeted us.

"He called round yesterday," I said. "Needing some company. Poor guy, he's stuck in some hotel while the police check the house. He's really down."

"Who can blame him."

"Yes, he was in pieces really. Feeling bad he didn't kiss her goodbye, kept thinking about the last things she said to him, her last words – checking he had his sandwiches. All a bit banal really as far as last words are concerned. Hope mine isn't 'Remember your packed supper, dear!'"

"Could have been worse. They might have been having a row, that might have been the last thing they said to each other, 'I hate you and always have!' 'Have you got your sandwiches' isn't too bad really by comparison."

"Is that what she said?"

"I don't know, something like that. I heard him answer her – 'Yes dear, I've got them', and he did – in a plastic box with a yellow lid. Awful to think if he hadn't gone out it wouldn't have happened. I expect he's thinking that too. At least now they've caught the killer his house will no longer be a crime scene and he'll be able to go home. Mind you, that will be difficult for him but better than being stuck in a hotel."

I wanted to say that Billy was probably lurking in his car parked nearby while all that conversation between us and Mr Fitzsimmons had happened but didn't want to have a row. We got our stews and Angela wanted to watch the film she needed to write about next on her course and I was keen to be obliging.

"What's it called?"

"*Gaslight*."

"*Gaslight*? What's that? A history of dimly-lit streets? Sounds rivetting!"

"No, it's one of the first psychological thrillers," she said, reading the box. "Odd name though."

We watched *Gaslight*. Angela read out her notes from the lecture: apparently this film, which seemed a bit far-fetched as well as a bit wooden in the acting department and afflicted with despair in that of costumes, had given rise to the term 'gaslighting' which, Angela read out, was now used to describe tricking someone into thinking they are misremembering something or misunderstanding something in a way that makes them start to doubt their own senses, which is, apparently, a technique used by abusers everywhere, but to me sounded like an adaptation of skills primarily used by the advertising industry.

"So when he goes in the loft and turns the lights down she thinks she's losing her mind and nobody listens to her?"

"Yes."

"I'm in the wrong job, I could write better plots than that! Anything else on?"

We sort of forgot about the stew and moved onto wine, coffee, and junk television as a concession to me to move away from old films for a change and harmony was restored, but just as we were settling down for an afternoon's telly and wine there was a knock at the back door.

Angela opened it. Standing on the backstep was a young woman with long, dark hair, a heart-shaped face,

253

wearing an Alice band and a bright red coat. She had a white dog with her on a lead. The dog panted excitedly, looking in at us. The young woman looked more wary. She raised her other hand and we saw she was carrying the newspaper we had left. We invited her in but she hesitated and remained on the doorstep.

"How did you get our address?" was the first thing I asked. I knew it hadn't been in the newspaper report and we had only left a mobile number with Leon. "When you said you'd call, we were expecting a phonecall. Have you come from London?" I was especially alarmed knowing she was part of a gang and I didn't know who else now had our address.

She shook her head. "No, London was all Leon could think of to put you off the scent as he didn't know how much trouble we might be in. He thought you were detectives. I told him he needn't worry, I haven't committed any crime. Private detective indeed, Mrs Crawford! You put the frighteners on me I must say, nearly dropped my phone when Leon texted me. I shouldn't use my phone at work so had to wait all shift to know more. Then no-one showed up to take over from me – we've been so short staffed since Covid – I was panicking I couldn't get away. But when I saw your photograph I knew you immediately, and the relief!" She had a broad smile which lit up her face. "But I came as quick as I could when I read this. There's no way this young lad had anything to do with it. We must get him released."

Angela was staring at her, mystified and alarmed. So was I. How on Earth did she know Angela's full name? We certainly had not divulged that. Even I would have had to think to recall her surname as I never referred to her as 'Mrs Crawford' so certainly hadn't used this name in Buttersville! I felt a net was closing in on us.

Anthea was telling us, as we gaped at her in panic, that Leon had surreptitiously taken photographs of each of us as we had sat in his room and sent them to her as soon as she had come off shift at the care home where she worked with the message, 'These two private detectives called today'.

"How do you know my name and address?" Angela was looking puzzled and quite fearful.

The young woman sighed and then pulled her heavy dark fringe off her face and held her face for inspection. "Do you know me now? I haven't changed that much, have I? It's been a while. I used to play with your Hugo and ... my name was different ... I was a lot smaller then. You haven't seen me for about 12 years, it was at a fete up on the common one year if you remember. I was with my parents then."

Angela stared open mouthed and then said, wonderingly, "Finley?"

Anthea let her hair drop back into place and gave a

sort of smile. "That was the name people gave me but *my* name is Anthea."

There was a pause.

"Do you still want me to come in?"

There was a moment's hesitation but 'of course ' was said.

She hesitated a moment as if unsure we meant it then she turned and waved to someone down on the road behind her. We heard a car start up and, looking through the kitchen window, I saw a blue-and-white car head off up the road towards the common.

"That was Leon dropping me off, he waited for my signal that I was okay here. He's going to meet his parents in town. He's not allowed at their house after everything but they meet up in a cafe now. He'll pick me up in an hour, or when I call. I wasn't sure how you'd … if I'd be …"

She was ushered in. Angela sat her down and fetched more coffee.

Anthea was looking around her. "It's been a while since I was in here, in my other life. It seems smaller!"

We did introductions.

"We never met," she said to me. "When I saw you up at the window that night I just assumed new people were living here."

We gave a brief resume: Martin moving out, me

moving in, separations and divorces and whatnot.

"Sorry for the delay, I had a double shift, then nearly a treble and then had to wait for Leon to be free to bring me. I didn't want to tell you it all on the phone. This is Cassie." The fluffy white dog wagged her tail, her tongue hanging out. She looked as if she knew we were talking about her. She looked very relaxed and happy and flopped down at Anthea's feet.

Angela fetched coffee and biscuits and there was a pause.

Chapter Sixteen

Lifestyle Choices

"I'll explain," said Anthea, "and I promise it will be the short version."

She took a biscuit and shared it with Cassie. She took a deep breath.

"Cassie is the daughter of my earlier friend, Duchess. Duchess was a pedigree breeding dog and show dog too. Duchess kept me company when I needed it. All the way from when I was about nine until I was 19. That was when I left home and took her with me. Cassie was still only a very young dog then so I left her. I couldn't take them both. Cassie and Duchess were both breeding dogs and show dogs for my parents. They are not loved, they are just money spinners, that's all. They didn't love Duchess and they didn't love me – that's just how it was. Some breeders care for their dogs some parents love their kids, others don't. It's just luck of the draw."

Her voice was very matter of fact. I felt she had shared this often enough for it to have become a part of her past and of no pain to her any more, or at least the scar tissue was thick enough to contain it. She took a delicate bite of her biscuit and ruffled Cassie's head.

"They told me I was a boy, but I always knew I was a girl. They tried to make me be a boy. I used to play with the other kids in the close. I think I was one of the youngest. Your Hugo was always like a big brother to me but then they kept me away from the other children from when I was about eight, in case somebody spotted how weird I was. I didn't think I was weird. I just felt I was a normal little girl, I just had the wrong plumbing, that was all. They were so worried about what the neighbours would think. The school told them I was causing problems – not wanting to do what boys are supposed to do – so they took me out of the school, the one on the common. It's closed now. As soon as I hit teen years they sent me to an all-boys' school 'to make a man of me' my dad said. I actually hoped it would, everything would be alright then, but not much chance of that!

"It was fairly hellish, even for the ones who *were* boys. Most of them just let me get on with being me but others didn't. I won't go into that. Some of the teachers too. That's when I started self-harming. It made the pain finite at least. I couldn't find anyone else like me. Then the school expelled me. Sent me 'home'. I was glad to be back with Duchess and Cassie but I was kept in all the time. Home schooled. That meant being shut in a room with some books, a laptop, and my dogs if I was good. The worst thing they could do was take them from me if I was naughty. I spent the time practising their signatures and looking up what I needed to know on the computer – planning my escape. And I used to sneak out at night. I expect Hugo has told you that. He probably saved my life – him and Duchess and Cassie."

Angela was gaping again and I gently used a finger to push her lower jaw upwards as the look did not suit her.

Anthea noticed and stumbled a little, "Oh maybe he hasn't, sorry, shouldn't have said …" She blushed and shifted in her chair.

"I used to go out at night and go into town to the clubs. I found a gay club eventually and felt something like at home there, although I knew it wasn't about being gay but my parents never knew about those outings. I came across the film *Little Big Man* online – that opened my eyes. I knew then that I wasn't a freak. I realised what I was and there are others like me, and there always have been people like me. I was so over the moon and grateful. I even sent Dustin Hoffman a card to say thank you to pass on to the actor who played the 'Twin Spirit' woman. I hope he got it. 'Twin Spirit' they called us – the First Nations – a lot better than some of the things I've been called! Then somebody I met at one of the clubs gave me a copy of *Tales of the City* and *The Danish Girl* and I was home and dry. I knew who I was.

"Then I saw Hugo playing in his band at one club. I recognised him at once when he introduced all the band, though I hadn't seen him for years and he was all grown up. He must have been about 18 then I suppose."

Angela made to interrupt but I touched her arm to prevent her, thinking other stories could wait. I had always meant to talk to her about the tree outside Hugo's window and the mystery of all that 'late night studying' he had done with the poor exam results he had achieved and how he had progressed into the musical world where he had built his career but had never got around to, probably because it wasn't my story.

"I was doing online education – like in Lockdown – then did an online course, Health and Beauty, and I passed. I ordered a brand new dress to celebrate. I was 19 by then. I think Hugo must have left for Canada by then so I was more alone than ever and when I came downstairs in my new dress my parents flipped out, they told me to get out and not come back. But I had already packed. I'd applied for a place on a college course and got accepted. They didn't even know. As long as I'd stayed out of sight they didn't take much interest. I'd eat my meals in my room and watched telly there. The college matched me up with another student needing a flatmate, I signed the social services letters confirming estrangement, forging their signatures, and I took Duchess with me. They didn't make a fuss that time. Duchess had just had her last litter and she would have been taken to the vets that year, so I left thinking I was saving her life but I was really saving mine. She was lonely too, having her puppies taken off her all the time."

Anthea stopped here and stroked Cassie a bit longer. I had heard about people being 'confused' about who they were or what gender they were but she didn't seem confused at all – she seemed to know exactly who she was. It was the world that seemed confused with its tidy categories and neat boxes that didn't really fit anyone.

"You don't have to tell us if it upsets you," I suggested, aware she was, silently, in tears.

"No, you need to know so you'll understand. That's nearly it now. I got on the course. The flatmate thing ended when the rent went up and my flatmate went back to her parents. I slept rough for a while – didn't tell the college – me and Duchess looking after each other – it was a mild winter thank god! I cut patches off her fur and put dye on some of it so no-one would see what she was and try and steal her. That's when I met Leon. He was sleeping rough too, couldn't cope with his family or ordinary life anymore. He's got PTSD, he's an ex-squaddie. The war did terrible things to him – screaming, nightmares, and flashbacks. He was on all sorts to kill the pain … heroin … his family couldn't cope. We looked after each other. I helped him get on a course at the college and he got counselling there too and started treatment. Then his nan offered him a room in her basement flat as long as he stayed clean and he brought me along. We have a room each. She was a bit put out when I came along but she's really nice. she never wanted him to join up and she knows Leon and I are friends and I support him. Then I changed course to Health and Social care, got a placement, got my certificate, now I work in the care homes in the area and they think I'm brilliant!

"Leon's got a really un-threatening job with a supermarket and he's still having counselling for PTSD. He lives in his wizarding world much of the time, it's much nicer than the one he's had to deal with. He's off the heroin and looks younger than he is – that's the steroids puffing his face out. I'm 27, he's a few years older. He's on steroids for the injuries. I'm just across the corridor if he has a difficult night. We look after each other really. I love working in the care homes. They love me. I look after them but they look after me twice as much – grandparents and parents I never had, and his nan too. I do their hair and nails and skin care and personal care and we talk and laugh. I hold their hands when nobody has visited, or when they have forgotten that somebody visited that very day, or when there is no-one to visit and they look forward to seeing me. They look after me more than I look after them. Covid took so many. It was … so difficult … like losing another family but we held together. Duchess got old; she'd had a good few years of being a dog instead of a commodity but I had to do the right thing by her and called the vet. She died in my arms.

"And then I knew I must come and get her daughter – Cassie – so I did. I wrote my parents a letter offering her a home but they said she wasn't old enough yet, still a breeder, a money spinner. They didn't mind me taking Duchess but Cassie was still an earner, so I … well you know the rest. I left a note to tell them what I'd done. There's no way they thought it was that young lad or anyone else. Yes I did steal her, but I see it as rescuing her from a life of misery."

"I saw the note," I said remembering. "You had it in your … right hand as you went down the drive."

Anthea smiled, "You spotted it. Well you and Leon can both witness that then if they deny it."

Angela poured her another coffee.

264

"Isn't child abuse against the law?" she said.

"They don't bother with leafy lanes," said Anthea. "Or if you've got the right accent. A lot of those kids I met at school had been sent there at the age of four. I think it messes them up. If that isn't abuse I don't know what is, and not a social worker in sight! So, anyway," Anthea sniffed and fetched out a flowered handkerchief to wipe her nose, "Leon was up for it. We were both free one night – his nan had always agreed I could keep a dog as long as I cleaned up after it – and the home agreed I could bring a therapy dog to work with me as long as I took full responsibility for her. Sorted. All I had to do was get here, use the window I'd used for years – I still have the penknife I used to use on my key ring. Dogs don't forget you, it had been years since Cassie had seen me. She and Duchess had always used to greet me when I got back after a night out and there she was again, like old times. She followed me out of the window like a trooper. She has to stay in the office a lot for now when I'm there but I'm doing the therapy-dog assessment with her next week and we'll be away. The residents love having a dog about the place and they'll adore Cassie – she's a natural. Be nice for her too, no more lonely days and no more losing her puppies!

"My parents know it was me who took the dog," she concluded. "There is no way they should have involved the police, that young man had nothing to do with it!" She took a sip of coffee and nodded her thanks. "I never thought they'd do all this. I'm sorry they did and that poor lad … he's a Traveller the paper said? Burglars must all throw their hats in the air when Travellers come to town 'cos they know whatever they do from then on will be pinned on the Travellers. They must have a field day, police too. Easy nicks for all!"

We interrupted her to reassure her that a lot was already proven and that the young lad was already released although the dog napping was still not solved.

"Did you break the window in the front door?"

"What?" she frowned delicately. "No, why would I? That side window has always been loose and it's quite easy to open it if you have a blade to start it off. I use my library card and a butter knife. You just push it shut when you've finished. I've been doing it for years and never even chipped a nail."

"So, why—?"

"Insurance," Anthea seemed quite clear what the motive would have been. "I expect Cassie's insured for more than ten or twenty grand. It's funny, when you've got money, it's never enough – you always want more. Maybe because it cannot give you what you need so you keep thinking 'oh if I just had another thirty grand, that'll do it'. My folks have got plenty but never enough. That's why I took her, rescued her. And they've pinned it on that lad. I came as soon as I knew. Thanks for leaving us that paper. It gave us both a shock. I couldn't believe it when I saw it! Cassie's mother and grandmother were my friends – all through my childhood. My horrible childhood. She had to have puppies every year and have them taken away. She would grieve every time and lose loads of weight. But then she'd have to do it again. We were company for each other."

Questions hung in the air.

"They said they didn't have a … son."

"Well they got that right! I always knew I was a girl but they wouldn't accept it. They think it's all about the plumbing, what bits you've got, but it isn't. It's who you know you are. When I behaved in ways they didn't like I got locked in my room for punishment." She smiled ruefully. "That's what you get with dogs – unconditional acceptance. She liked me, she didn't care what plumbing I'd been born with. I think animals know, y'know, the Spirit lives in the heart, not the genitalia, if you don't mind me mentioning …" She had blushed.

Angela offered her another biscuit.

"Nice lad, your Hugo," said Anthea. "He helped me too. How is he doing now? He must be what …?"

"33 this year. He's fine thanks, married with kids."

Anthea dunked her biscuit delicately in her coffee and caught it like an expert at the crucial point between nicely soaked and sodden and broken. I'd always admired that skill.

"I'm glad he's okay. He was a friend too, in my teens, when I needed all the support I could get. Sneaking out at night kept me sane. At least I could meet others … like me … or a bit like me."

"Maybe that's all any of us meet," Angela said thoughtfully and we nodded, thinking of all the people we had met who were a bit like ourselves but not very.

"And Mr Crawford? Where's he?" said Anthea, her brow furrowed.

"Martin? He decided he was gay," said Angela, abruptly, "left me for somebody else."

"Oh!" said Anthea, surprised.

"Yeh, it was a bit 'Oh!'" agreed Angela. "It's better now. I realised it wasn't my 'fault', I didn't 'make him gay' and it isn't a 'lifestyle choice' either," said Angela. "We've talked a bit. And I know his family. He was brought up to believe gay people were dangerous, that they molested children, attacked people, raped people, and weren't really people in the full sense of the word. His dad was *very* clear about it. It took Martin a little bit of time to work his way through that lot. He found out he was one of the people his parents had always warned him about."

"Yeah, funny, that's what they say about us transfolk now. Oh well, at least they're consistent," she counted on her fingers. "Everybody they don't like are ... 1) a danger to children; 2) violent and a threat to others; 3) rapists and 4) not really human. Oh yes, and 5) they always carry diseases, nearly forgot that one. Are you okay though? That must have hurt you."

"I'm better now. I think I'm beginning to understand better. We could be friends, after a while. He loved me but not like that, it's not his fault."

"Lots of different ways of loving people," commented Anthea, "and most aren't 'like that'. I think Leon and I love each other but not like that. We're just not each others' type and we've been friends for too long. Complicated, isn't it?"

"So what now?" I said.

Chapter Seventeen

Going Home

"I'm not giving Cassie back, I'm not betraying her. She's got a good life with me, well, at least she's got a life."

"Will your parents charge you with theft? Breaking and entering?"

"They might."

"But would the police touch it? 'Estranged child comes back for pet dog'. Not exactly Scotland Yard material, is it?" I mused.

"I have to sort it out or it'll stay as an open case, then when someone else gets arrested they'll ask them to admit to it as part of a deal for a lighter sentence."

We must have gaped a little because Anthea said, "You do learn a bit living on the streets, you hear people's stories of how they got there. Those kinds of deals can mean shorter sentences, sometimes."

I thought of Billy, 'other crimes to be taken into consideration', among them a dog-napping and maybe a few other burglaries the police had not solved. If he admitted to them his sentence would be lighter, maybe. The police clean-up rate looks better – everyone's a winner. Especially the actual criminal of those 'other crimes' whom nobody will bother looking for any more.

"But then your mum and dad might just press charges against you?"

I had an idea.

"I'm going to make a phone call. Angela, you've got the number."

And so it was that, later that day, Angela, Anthea, Cassie the dog, and myself were heading out to the Harrisons' abode.

"Ooh it's like *High Noon*," enthused Angela. "Except for the dog, they didn't have a dog in *High Noon*, only horses."

"You like films too?" said Anthea as we stepped out of the porch. "Have you seen *Pride*?"

"Oh yes," said Angela, "brilliant – I miss disco too! But it *was* all a bit far-fetched!"

Anthea looked surprised, "No, it was all a true story. It all happened!"

Angela looked surprised this time as we headed down the driveway.

"I wish," continued Anthea, as we started across the road, "that someone would make a film about Stonewall, then transfolk could be the stars."

I could see that Angela wanted to ask what Stonewall meant but just as she opened her mouth a policeman got out of the car which had pulled up at the top of the Harrisons' drive a few minutes previously. It was our Plum.

He acknowledged us and fell into stride alongside us as we arrived at the Harrisons' front door, which was beginning to look very familiar to me as it was the third visit this week. Cassie pulled back on her lead all the way down the drive, as if not wanting to go to the house, but whined and crept along behind Anthea's legs. Anthea gently stroked and reassured her into calmness but Cassie kept up a quiet whimper for all the time we were near the door.

Two cars were in the driveway, showing that the Harrisons were probably at home. It might have appeared to be an amazing coincidence that a policeman we recognised, even though he was out of uniform, arrived at the same time and in what appeared to be his own car. My 'urgent' message left at the station had apparently been passed on to the particular police officer whom I had specified and, despite being off duty and despite a missing dog not being the station's current top priority, he had come running. Evidently a true dog-lover and passionate law-enforcer, keen to see the just outcome of this intriguing case.

My message had said that the missing dog would be returned to its rightful home at 6 p.m. this evening and here he was right on time.

The PC, our Plum, had just been getting out of his car as we arrived at the top of the Harrisons' drive, which might have seemed another amazing coincidence but which only occurred because we had all been crowded into Angela's front porch and looking out of its window for a car with him in it to arrive before all setting off for our visit, so arriving at the Harrisons' front door in one big friendly bunch. The only one among us not keen on our direction of travel seemed to be Cassie.

"So this is the dog?" said Plum, as we stood at the new front door and he pressed the bell with authority, looking at Anthea. "They'll be pleased to get her back, And you are?"

"I'm their daughter, Anthea," she said and was going to say more but at that point the door opened and we were once again in the presence of Joan and Charles, neither of whom went into raptures at the sight of any of the group gathered on their doorstep.

The dog at this point began whining and tried to run back up the drive to the end of its lead, turning at its end and twisting her head in an attempt to escape the collar. Anthea went to her, all reassurances and comforting sounds. Cassie lay down at Anthea's feet, looking up at her with a world of anxiety in her eyes, tail wagging furiously, trying to earn forgiveness for whatever dreadful crime she had committed which had urged this awful punishment.

Plum looked from Cassie to the Harrisons who were watching implacably.

"This your dog?" he said and there was indeed a shade of doubt in his voice, evidence of significant powers of observation.

"Yes," said Charles, who obviously had no idea when he was beat and stepped forward, reaching out his hand to Anthea for the lead, but that was enough for Cassie to take matters into her own paws, backing up the drive away from him, barking. It was the first time we had heard her bark. Charles gave up and went back to his wife's side. They stood there looking unhappy.

Anthea, having calmed Cassie down, said, "I'm sorry you thought someone had stolen her. I left a note explaining that I'd come to take her back with me. I think she belongs with me, I've got a flat now," she said to the officer. "My parents and I have been estranged for a while now, you see—"

"A note?" said the officer, one eyebrow raised, looking hard at the Harrisons. "A family tiff and a note?"

"Well we didn't get a note!" said Joan and Charles together.

"Oh I saw her delivering it, on the night in question. I was watching from that window," I pointed.

"And my friend who was the driver saw me deliver it too," said Anthea.

There was a moment of quiet. Plum folded his arms and looked at the Harrisons.

"Maybe it got lost under the mat, like the note in *Tess of the D'Urbervilles*?" offered Angela, always one to find the way to peace.

Everybody watched as Mr Harrison tried to pull up the carpet inside the bottom of the door frame but it was top-quality, heavy wool twist, had been laid by a professional and wasn't going to come loose with anything less than a crowbar and certainly not for any mere piece of paper dropping through the post-box.

"Maybe the dog ate it?" Angela suggested, brightly.

The Harrisons grasped at the idea and hummed and nodded and looked again at Cassie who again began barking nervously and Joan recounted how Cassie 'sometimes did eat the mail – naughty dog!'

"Yes, or maybe it just burst into flames," said Plum, who was still looking at the Harrisons with a fixed expression which was neither one of adoration or chum-ship.

"Okay, let's say the dog ate it," he said. "And you thought your dog had been stolen, but it was only a mistake So, unless you want to press charges against your own daughter for breaking and entering, there's no crime here."

Joan and Charles looked as if they'd like to do just that, and a whole lot more besides, but just looked sulky.

"Yes, Officer," said Anthea, "all a horrible mistake. It was my pet dog and I came to take her away. Just a family squabble. Here's the dog, not stolen at all. They didn't find my note, maybe it blew in the fire? We're here to make amends and look, we're reconciled and it's all over. It was my dog, I just came to fetch her."

"You pleased your daughter's brought the dog back?"

"She's not ... yes, Officer," said Charles, trying to look pleased but only managing to look constipated.

Plum frowned at Anthea, "Well, young lady, you've caused a deal of trouble."

"I'm so sorry, Officer," murmured Anthea in a melodic voice and I'm not sure she didn't flutter her eyelashes at him in a way I'd never been able to achieve.

"Why didn't you just ring the bell? Breaking the window! Er … or climbing through a window, whichever it was you did," said Plum.

I remembered the saying that liars need to have good memories, or at least carry a notebook at all times.

"I'm sorry, we're estranged and I just didn't want to see them. I'm sorry. I'll pay for the damage."

Angela looked as if she wanted to mention the side-window which hadn't needed to be broken and which was easy to get into and out of but we both kept quiet. This was Anthea's gig and she had her reasons.

"So, this is your pet dog?" said the policeman.

The dog had kept leaping up at Anthea in a show of doggy adoration so the question seemed to be redundant.

The officer came to a decision.

"Right, the young lad we arrested has been released anyway,' (this sounded like a source of personal grief to himself), 'and a lot of paperwork done. But the dog is safe – not stolen. It's a family affair, a squabble, nothing for us to do, and so this is no longer registered as a crime. I will note it as resolved and the crime number I gave you is now obsolete. I will leave it to you to notify the insurance company of that and to close the claim. I do hope you haven't already spent some of that money." He said this last sentence in a kind of flat voice, accompanied with a flat stare at Joan and Charles.

The Harrisons both looked a bit stricken and looked at him.

"We have actually," said Charles. "About half! But I would hope we *would* be able to get some of that back." There seemed to be a hint in his voice.

Charles and Joan both stared at Plum who shrugged in response then got out his car keys and started to head back up the drive.

"Well that's unfortunate, expensive times these, but at least you haven't been the victim of a crime, nor has anyone said anything about, er, let's see, wasting police time; suspicion of fraud or attempted fraud; defamation of character; perverting the course of justice; providing false information to police in the course of their duty; and behaviour likely to lead to affray and disturbance of the peace – with meetings up on the common maybe designed to incite hatred …" He was halfway up the drive and turned for a parting shot. "I'll see what my superiors say about all that. Goodbye."

"That was just to oblige a good friend and return a favour," called out Charles, stepping out of the door and making as if to catch up with Plum and reason with him but Plum was getting into his car and made no response before driving off.

Joan had turned even whiter than usual. She followed her husband out of the door, looked to him in panic but he shook his head slightly and patted her arm in reassurance. We all knew that Plum's superiors weren't going to be the slightest bit interested in 'all that'.

"Another case cleared up, they're doing well," Angela said, cheerfully.

"Well at least Plum is, very well, *and* the Police Benevolent Fund," I added.

There was a silence. Mr H's eyes seemed to bulge and Mrs H was staring at Anthea as if she was looking at an alien.

"Are you going to invite me in?" asked Anthea, softly. There was an appeal in her voice.

In answer, Charles looked at Angela and me with a glare and began to turn back towards the door. Joan was already halfway there. "You've done enough harm here today," he snarled in our directions and she backed this up with a glare. "Leave our property, if you please."

Neither of them looked at Anthea or responded to her plea. They reached the doorway and walked back inside the house. Anthea stepped forward, as if to follow them in, but Joan, quite firmly and looking straight at Anthea, took hold of the door and shut it in her face.

Anthea stood looking at the closed door, biting her lip, then she reached down to Cassie who was sitting at her feet, looking up at her, and gave the dog a fuss and a hug, burying her face in the white fur.

"Come on," said Angela, "coffee at our place. And biscuits too." She took Anthea's arm in hers as if brooking no refusal and turned her decisively away from the closed door. We all walked back up the drive and into our house, the fluffy white dog gambolling and pulling on the lead in front the whole way.

"I need to think about something else – something good. My counsellor at college taught me to do this. It's otters playing – I always think about otters playing – it makes the memories go away." Anthea was telling Angela.

"It was obviously an insurance job," Anthea was saying, later after a good cry and a shoulder rub and lots of thinking of 'otters playing'. "If I told the insurance company what really happened, they'd be done for fraud, but even that's a civil matter, not criminal I think. Anyway, if all they want in life is money then let them have it – they've got nothing I want or need." She accepted a mug of hot chocolate and another biccie.

"What if they get another dog?" I said. "They've fixed the window now."

"Let me know if they do," said Anthea. "There's always bricks!"

We smiled. "And I know someone who could lend us a sledgehammer if a brick's not enough," I added.

"Thanks, I didn't want them to be in a load of trouble. I just want to leave it and them behind. I'd better ring Leon, he'll be wondering what's happened to me. It'd be nice if he can meet you and know you are not private detectives on his trail, poor lad, he had a bit of an attack when you told him that."

"We'll be having a Skype with Hugo on Monday night again, would you like to come and join in if you can get here? Or we can fill him in? He'll be pleased to know you're alright."

"That'd be nice. I'll ask about my shifts. If not, maybe another time?"

This was said shyly and warily.

"Never mind 'maybe'," said Angela. "There's always enough coffee going for one more and besides," she hesitated a moment, then took Anthea's hand, "Hugo always wanted a sister, and I never had a daughter, so you call here whenever you want a bit of home life, and bring Leon too! He's got a mum and dad and a nan but maybe I can be his auntie."

Anthea didn't answer, her eyes full of tears again as Angela held her and hugged her and said, "There, there!"

Which got me thinking …

Chapter Eighteen

Looking For Eric

The usual self-satisfied peace of the early hours of Monday morning in a houseful of the self-employed and semi-retired was shattered by some escapee from Hell ringing the doorbell as if anything in Life could possibly be more important than the extra half hour's kip which body and soul demanded. Daylight had only recently begun to nervously arrive so I lay there hoping they'd either go away or die but it rang again. I heard Angela leave her room and go downstairs, muttering. Thinking it might be the police with an update I hauled myself heroically out of the snuggled warmth and into my dressing gown while hunting down my slippers which were lurking in the shadows, looking as disgruntled as I was at the early onset of action.

But outside there was a milkman, looking apologetic and tired. He was carrying some cartons of milk and a box of eggs which he sort of waved at us as we peered out at him through the kitchen door like knights of old in a medieval castle might have looked out at a marauding horde come knocking at the drawbridge. We were both trying to figure out what was happening. This time of the morning was not something we did, I'm happy to say, or had ever done.

Eventually, Angela opened the door. The milkman said that he was awfully sorry but that next door was still a crime scene and he didn't know what to do with the milk order. We must have looked a bit blank. He went on to ask if he could leave it here and we nodded as that seemed reasonable. He handed over the milk and the eggs then started to ramble, "I don't want him to miss his milk and eggs on top of everything. I don't even know if he's there or not, that tape is everywhere. I can't go in that garden again, I *can't* go in there … Does he want his milk and eggs or was it only Mrs Fitzsimmons, poor lady, who drank milk and ate eggs? Do you know? I don't …I don't know!"

Angela invited him in for a cup of tea and in he came with all his stress and woe even though it was still only seven in the morning.

"Last time I went in there …" and then I realised, of course, he was the one who had found the body. This was the milkie who had gone round the back of the house on Friday morning and found our neighbour Edith dead in her garden

"She'd been killed with the hedge-trimmer. It was lying there, one of those portable ones—"

"Oh yes, I know," said Angela, "they're very handy they are, I've always …"

He looked at her helplessly.

"Do you want to talk about it?" said Angela, backtracking and, despite all my hard staring, indeed he did. Angela showed him into the living room and sat him down even though he was in his work-clothes. She didn't even remember to put a newspaper under him.

He told us what he had found: Mrs Fitzsimmons, who had apparently been a good customer for years, had been lying dead on the path by the hedge and 'there was blood everywhere', on the path, on the hedge-trimmer lying close by, and on the white coverall she was wearing, 'like some people do to protect their clothes when gardening'. He really didn't want to go in that house again. He'd only gone in there to put the refuse bags back safely. He had never seen a dead body before, not since his mother had passed and that was peaceful, not all covered in blood, and they had expected it for a while, with she being 97 and all and a heavy smoker to the last.

He was obviously very upset and traumatised by the whole experience so I knew it was going to take a while to get rid of him. I mumbled an excuse, left him to Angela, and wandered into the kitchen to make coffee. Waiting for the kettle to boil, I spotted the small blue bowl of flowers still on the window sill. They had wilted and most had died, their petals and leaves either fallen on the sill or hanging over the edge of the bowl; drooping like a little visual metaphor for the brevity of life and its fleeting moment, although probably made a darn sight more fleeting by being cut off at the roots and bunged into a little bowl of water then neglected on somebody's window sill, I had to acknowledge. I picked up the little bowl of dead or dying flowers and leaves. Feeling guilty, I opened the food-waste caddy on the draining board and clumsily dropped them in, closing the lid. One stalk stuck out from under the lid, it drooped over the edge, its stem brushing its sides, leaving a few drops of water on the green paint … and that was when it all hit me …

… she was wearing one of those cotton coveralls over her clothes …

… leaves hanging over the side …

… there was blood everywhere …

… that wussy stuff Billy-boy's been doing.

… they'd been gardening all day….

… there was blood everywhere…

His suit looked slightly crumpled as if it had been

in a suitcase.

I didn't really hear anything to be honest, my hearing is not good.

… this is real recycling …

… then, as if my mind had spent days desperately hunting for the right file amongst the infinite ranks of filing cabinets full of old junk, lost dreams, and unnecessary memories which I laughingly call a brain, one memory was found and was hurled across the chasm between unconscious and conscious and stood in the full blazing light of all of my attention…

… It was the scene of last Thursday evening; Angela and myself standing chatting and half-listening to Mr Fitzsimmons on the pavement by our several bags of assorted items for recycling. The collection truck – or van as some might call it – was coming back down the cul-de-sac, the crew members were dodging back and forth, heaving up the sacks of green and white, carrying them to the truck and throwing them aboard. Most of them were wearing hi-vis yellow jackets but one was only wearing ordinary clothes as if this wasn't his real job and he hadn't come prepared or had a proper induction. He was wearing a red, checked shirt. Then, in my mind's eye, Angela and I turned to go back in the house and Mr Fitzsimmons had driven off in his car but the action continued and the man in the red, checked shirt – not in the full fount of youth, already wearing on his face some lines of care and of parenthood's many worries, of getting by and of life's pressures – picked up the full white bags left by Mr Fitzsimmons and heaved them onto his shoulder where little trailing leaves of laburnum, forsythia, and leylandi hedge-cuttings gently brushed their miniscule specks of treason onto the worn cotton and left it there, as if plotting revenge for their own demise and grisly end…

The scene wound backwards to a little earlier the same day. Mr Fitzsimmons was upstairs in his own house rushing to put on a smart brown suit and shoes, replacing shorts and a vest top he had been wearing until now; then he hurriedly pulled a white, cotton coverall back on over all his clothes and shoes, fastened the velcro at the front on his way back downstairs, back out to the garden where his wife was beginning to pile some of the chopped leaves and twigs they had cut from the hedge into the garden-waste bags.

He took a brief detour on the way to pass by the garden gate to peek out through its black metal bars to check – yes they were still there and on schedule, the two neighbours who always were there at this time of a Thursday evening for the waste truck's arrival. Then, hurrying now, back past the edge of the BBQ, which was still smouldering after their afternoon 'so impromptu' afternoon late lunch a la fresco which Edith, poor fool, had thought so romantic, and picked up the heavy-duty hedge-trimmer he had put there on his way into the house. He picked it up and headed, more quickly now and not breathing, towards where Edith bent and straightened, bent and straightened. Sensing his arrival, she began to turn just as he raised the trimmer and brought it crashing down, once, twice, on the back of her coiffured head and she fell.

Had she turned a little earlier, had their eyes met, would it have stayed his hand? Would that have brought to his mind their decades of togetherness, their first meeting, the birth of their children ... would that have momentarily doused the thoughts of the life insurance and of his new lover, and the greed for the promise of their new and opulent life together? But their eyes did not meet and Edith fell. Her eyes closed forever and he had done what could never be undone.

He stood for a second. He was in shock at the amount of blood. It was everywhere. Then he congratulated himself on the forethought and planning which meant none of it would be found on him. Check the pulse – nothing. But now the crucial part, the difficult part, the alibi, and he had only minutes to secure it. Off with the blood-spattered cotton coverall and gloves, tearing the thin cotton into the BBQ to re-stoke the friendly flames. Quickly grab up handful after handful of the prunings to fill the bags to make it look real, take them in one hand and, out of the shelf below the BBQ where it had sat hidden since last night, the plastic box of sandwiches for his train journey and the small overnight case, then out to the front drive, keys in his suit jacket – ooh! nearly forgot! Quick check in the hand mirror of the compact he had put in his suit pocket yesterday, a few specks of the blood on his face soon wiped off with his handkerchief. That goes onto the BBQ too, burning nicely now. Can't be too careful. Then, out to the front, like any good neighbour, in a rush from gardening, off to keep an appointment, meet with old comrades, celebrate a birthday. Tiresome really, pity Edith was not up to it; make sure they notice the time, make sure they notice the smart, spotless suit, make sure they hear his conversation with Edith – or think they do. It was a technique he had used with Edith over the years, showing surprise at her not remembering a detail he had never told her, concerns at her loss of memory when she caught him in a lie, frustration that the doctor would do nothing to help with her failing recall when he had to change arrangements with his lover at the last minute … or when Edith began to suspect…

"Beth? You okay?" Angela was walking the milkman, Gordon, to the door and waving him goodbye. She was holding the milk and eggs he had left in our charge. He looked more cheerful and headed off towards his milk float in the driveway.

I was still standing at the kitchen sink holding an empty blue bowl over the waste-food caddy and staring out of the window with my mouth half open. I turned to look at Angela. She could see immediately that I was far from 'okay'.

"Angie, I've made a terrible mistake!"

"Oh come here, that's okay, cut flowers don't last long whatever you do. Here."

She went to relieve me of the empty bowl, close the waste caddy, and comfort me.

"No, I didn't mean—" But just then there was a knock at the back door. Mr Fitzsimmons was standing on the doorstep. Angela hurried to open the door and asked him in, her voice full of empathy and commiseration as she offered him tea and I heard him say, "I'm sorry to call in so early but I saw Gordon was here and thought you might be up." He came in and his mouth smiled at us both as Angela gushed with reassurance that of course he was welcome any time and wouldn't he take a seat in the lounge and join us for breakfast while I somewhat gaped in silence.

"Oh I can't stay long," he was saying against Angela's insistence of hospitality. How long does it take, I thought, and glanced at his hands to see if he had any garden implements about him. Angela showed him into the sitting room and came back to put the kettle on again. He was saying he had not been able to sleep and came to the close 'to deliver these', showing us some envelopes with a black edging.

"Are you sure you're alright?" Angela said in the kitchen, fussing about the biscuit tin and glancing at me with my bowl of wilted flowers.

"Don't give him biscuits," I whispered.

"What?"

"He'll leave sooner if you don't—"

"Well that's a bit mean. He has just lost his wife!"

"We need to talk," I whispered.

Then Mr Fitzsimmons reappeared in our midst and I stopped whispering.

"I don't want to be rude but I can't stay for tea, thank you, just posting these invitations. Gives me something to do. How *was* Gordon? Did he say anything about … poor man, must have been a terrible shock … anything new? No? Well, I'm due to collect my keys from the police station this afternoon. It's going to no longer be a crime scene once all the reports are in – the suspect has actually admitted to working in the area which puts him at the scene of the crime of course, so that's that. Theft seems to have been the motive *and* he's got a record apparently. So, there'll be a trial of course but it seems cut and dried. I only wanted to call in to invite you, if you would be so kind," he hesitated, as one who approaches a delicate subject. "It's Edith's funeral on Wednesday. It would mean so much to me if you could come – you were there in her last hours and heard her final words if you remember, I'm sure you do. Caring about me as always. It would mean a lot to me and I'm sure she would want you to be there, our neighbours, and maybe Martin as well, if that would not be awkward, as he was our neighbour too. Time to forgive and so on?"

He seemed to imply that it was he who would be forgiving Martin. I swallowed the response that Martin may well wish to visit her grave at some point but probably not to adorn it, at least not with flowers, given their spiteful comments at his expense at their last encounter, so I struggled to find an acceptable reply but Angela was already there with "Of course we'd be delighted to come. Well, not delighted exactly, but pleased, well perhaps not pleased. Beth?" She looked to me for help.

"Of course we'll come, thank you for the invitation," I managed as the response most likely to oil his way to the door most effectively.

His face brightened. "Thank you. I've called down to invite some of the neighbours I'm but not ready to face them yet so I'm being the postie before they're up. The Harrisons of course and one or two others, you'll know people there, most of the Golf Club crowd. They'll be delighted to see you again I'm sure, though not, of course, in … present circumstances."

My smile was beginning to hurt and I couldn't stop looking at his hands, envisaging their actions of a few days previously. How clean and well manicured they looked!

"Well that'll be all then. I know we … er … drifted apart lately but hopefully this tragedy might reap some positives and bring us closer together. Oh! By the way, have you made a statement to the police yet about what you saw and heard?" he asked, as if it was a last-minute thought as he arrived back on the doorstep.

"Yes, we both did," Angela said, nodding. He looked pleased and headed for the door.

"I'll go and deliver the rest, and the police have called – they want to update me, they left a   message."

Then he was gone.

"Well that's nice," said Angela, looking at the invitation, the card all lilies and hands at prayer.

"Angie, *do* you remember Edith calling to him from the back garden? *Do* you remember what she said?"

"Well something about his sandwiches, I guess. That's what he answered!"

"Don't guess! That's what the brain does – it fills

in the gaps, it guesses the rest. Impressionist painters use the same technique – they *suggest* a sunset with a few red blobs and your brain makes it a sunset! What did you *hear* her say?"

"Sunset? Oh, um, well … to be honest … I didn't *hear* anything she said, but I assumed it was just my hearing being a bit dippy these days because *he* heard it and so did you, didn't you?"

"No! That's the point. I wasn't really paying that much attention as he was waffling on about his party, so that's why I thought I must have just missed hearing her call anything, but, Angela, I *didn't* hear anything. Honestly I didn't. Like you, I just thought she *must* have called out the question because he shouted out the answer – my mind *told* me she had called out to him! And he's called here twice now to make sure it worked!"

"What worked?"

"It's the trick, it's the 'gaslighting' – you know, make people think they have misheard or forgotten when they haven't!"

"So he must have heard it then? He's got better hearing!"

"No Angie, my hearing is fine and so is yours, we didn't hear anything because she didn't call anything. He didn't either, he was just pretending. She didn't call anything out because she was already dead. He came to us all chatty and friendly not because he was being neighbourly but because he was setting an alibi. I know how that blood got on Billy's shirt – he's not the killer. Edith's murderer just walked out of our kitchen."

Sometime later, by which time Angela looked as stricken as I did and we had locked the front and back doors against any further visitations by our friendly neighbour, we were dithering as to what to do next.

"We said in our statements that we heard her."

"We thought we had, we assumed."

Assumptions again.

"We have to contact the police and tell them we retract and we were wrong – we were tricked and we know now how the blood must have got on Billy's shirt and they've got the wrong man!"

"But how can we prove it, how can anybody prove it? 'We thought we heard her but now we think we didn't'? How far is that going to get us? They already think we're loopy, they'll lock *us* up too!"

"The fact we didn't hear her voice changes the parameters of when her death could have happened, it puts him in the frame. It was only our statements that kept him out of it … that she was alive when he left."

"Still no proof but they've got actual blood spots on Billy's shirt, they've got a body and the weapon *and* motive about his probably casing the joint, he's got a record of thieving. All we've got is possibly some blood on some plants that are long gone, they must be totally composted by now or shredded. Everything else burned."

Then Angela looked up, wide-eyed, "Beth – the bags! The milkie put the bags back. If the blood was on the leaves some of it might have got on the bags! If they're still in the garden …?"

"Oh yes, but no! The police have been all over that house and garden. They would have found the bags and any blood on them."

"Not if they weren't looking for them, why would they?"

"We've got to go and look, see if they're still there. They're white so any blood would show up, even without a microscope maybe—"

"Oh my god, Beth! Listen, Billy will have told the police he was working on the recycling truck that night, why wouldn't he, the police will have questioned him about his movements that night and he'd have told them and *the police will tell Mr Fitzsimmons*. They see it as just placing him at the scene of the crime, casing the joint as they suspected, but Fitzsimmons *knows* Billy is innocent. He'll be trying to figure out how the blood got on his shirt, as soon as he knows Billy was doing the recycling he'll realise—"

"And he'll know the bags could give him away, if he figures it out, which he will. It won't take him long. Before we can convince the police to take a second look anyway!"

"Do you think they have already told him? He might have gone there already to get them, burn them …?"

"He didn't say anything about it, just that the suspect 'was working in the area'. He doesn't know yet it was the waste truck or he'd have said so but as soon as he does he'll twig it. The police don't suspect him so they'll tell him the whole story."

"Billy was only arrested yesterday, he'd have been questioned, he'd have told them what he was doing. They would have checked his story, he's got alibis on the van but only until they finished, then he's got alibis at the meeting – us for one – but he's got no alibi for later when he went on the common to sleep. Liam they wouldn't listen to as they're cousins. They think Edith was killed some time between 6.30 when Mr F left and three in the morning. If there's any blood on those bags it would prove that she was dead before he put them on the pavement, if blood is on them, and proved Billy *couldn't* have done it and Mr

Fitzsimmons *had* to have. Oh god, what if there's no blood on them or he's taken them already?"

"He said he had a message to phone the police for an update, maybe that means they haven't told him yet what Billy told them. As soon as they do he'll know …"

"What will he do?"

"He'll be desperate to destroy those bags in case there's any evidence on them."

"He might already know, he might have seen Billy doing the recycling collection?"

"No he wouldn't, nobody notices who's collecting the rubbish. I didn't, only in the back of my mind. We need a plan. We could go and get them out of the garden and take them to the police."

"I think that's 'meddling with evidence' or something and they'll say we wiped some of the leaves that are still there onto them or something. No, we can't do that."

"I'll ring the police anyway – tell them we retract our statements and need to make new ones and that we've remembered details we'd forgotten about."

"Is it PC Plum who's running the case? He'll be impressed."

The officer I spoke to wrote down what I told him and said he would pass it on as soon as the detective in charge was available as he was 'on another call right now.'

I knew he'd be on the phone to Mr Fitzsimmons, assuring him of progress and telling him the suspect had admitted to being in the area on the day of the murder and of having no alibi during the time of the murder. Had they told them of Billy working on the recycling van, as a cover for his casing of possible thefts, as they would see it, and would Mr F take long to put two and two together and realise how that blood had got onto that shirt and where the risk now was to his story?

We went upstairs to the window to peer over the hedge and then outside to try and listen to see if Mr F was in his garden or if we could see the white bags somewhere but there was no sign.

"What are we going to do?"

It felt desperate. An innocent man was going to be convicted of murder and we had helped that to happen.

"I feel helpless," I said.

"Do you remember that film?" said Angela.

"Oh, Angela, not now, surely!"

"*Looking for Eric*. Remember that line?"

"I remember a lot of swearing."

"No, remember that one line – we need it now."

"What line?"

"'You must trust your friends' ... Beth, *we* must trust our friends!"

"But who *are* our friends?" I asked weakly.

"I've got a plan," said Angela.

A little while later, we made some more phone calls.

Chapter Nineteen

Gardening

Later, and it felt like much, much later, that afternoon, as the sun was getting low in the sky and the shadows were lengthening, Mr F drew up to his house in his car, got out, and walked across the drive. The black-and-yellow tapes were still in place but the detective in charge had told him he could by-pass them before they got officially removed, 'given the circumstances' that the killer was in custody, the evidence irrefutable, and no reason for him to be any more inconvenienced, sir.

He didn't go to the front door but stepped over the tape, across the garden gate, took out a bunch of keys, and unlocked the padlock on the gate. The garden was unusually quiet with no birdsong. Most of the garden was in shadow except for highlights of late sun on one side of each of its many bushes and trees.

He spotted the white bundle of garden-waste bags under the all-weather bench by the BBQ. The milkie must have stuffed them there, safe and sound and unlikely to be blown about again, before turning to make his terrible discovery. Mr F did not look behind him at the little enclave behind the magnolia where the chalked, white outline of a human shape could still be seen among scattered twigs and leaves on the pathway. He pulled the pile of white bags further into the centre of the paved patio so as to not set the garden alight and took a box of matches out of his trouser pocket. He reached under the BBQ stand and pulled out the bottle of lighter fuel that was kept there, opened it, and upended it over the pile of bags. He put it down when it was empty and lit a match.

Too late he heard the running footsteps, one set of rather lurching, uneven footsteps among others, heard the snap and flash of a camera then a body hit his in a rugby tackle which sent him crashing to the ground while a fist closed around the match, extinguishing its brief flame. A pain shot up his arm as it was wrenched behind him and his face introduced to the patio. One body held him down while another seemed to sit on his legs while a voice shouted "Citizen's arrest!" and suddenly there were footsteps of many people he couldn't see all over the garden emerging from behind bushes, trees, and trellises. Mr F yelled in shock and anger and pain, telling the unseen persons to 'get off me!' with various words not the kind often heard in the close as he realised why there were no birds in the garden this afternoon.

I got on my phone, as planned, and dialled 999, asked for police and told the officer the situation and its urgency as coherently as I could as Angela helped Liam with tying Mr F's shoe laces together and Matthew held him down on the floor with one hand while dexterously tying a rope around his hands with another. Mr F was struggling, "You have no right to be here – this is trespass! I'll charge you all with assault. You're not police, you have no powers—"

"If you're wondering what powers I've got, mister," said Matthew, in a calm voice, "you just keep struggling and you might find out."

Mr F became more still then went on, "You're hurting me. You have no right—"

Then Liam, pulling the laces into a firm knot and, reaching past Matthew to take hold of Mr F's hair to get his full attention, said, "Listen, I'm a trained boxer. I was picked for this job because I can keep my cool, even though it's my cousin and my chavvy you've had put in jail, but Matthew here is *not* a trained boxer so you just keep calm in case you rile him and, by the way," he tightened his grip momentarily, "if it's hurting you're worried about, you just be thankful we didn't bring Billy's mother or his missus because they don't play by the Queensbury rules either – so you lie quiet!" He let go of the hair.

Mr F seemed to hear this and was quieter. The photographer was taking more pictures of the bags from all angles in case of mishap and of the arrest, Liam pointing to his newly re-dyed hair and saying something about his 'best side' while Geraint was making notes of the scoop of the year. Angela and Liam had finished tying his feet together and, pulling some twine out of his pocket, started tying his legs. Everyone looked a bit tousled and leafy after our crawl through the hastily cut hole in the hedge between the two gardens.

Mr F seemed to get second wind and yelled, "It's you bloody pykies! I'll charge you all with trespass and assault." Matthew got up at this, his face tense, and Liam quickly took his place while I sat next to Angela, sitting on his back and tying twine, as Matthew needed some time out to walk about the garden and let off some steam. Mr F carried on in the same vein for a minute but then Liam found a handkerchief in Mr F's pocket and stuffed it in his mouth, saying, "That's quite enough from you, if you don't mind."

Liam said to me, "Matthew's son got called that at his last school, and then got charged with 'anti-social behaviour' because he socked the other kids, one each, so it makes him a bit cross."

I began to think maybe Mr F wasn't so bright for all his executive status, using the most foul racist term he could think of in present circumstances. Matthew came back and we swapped places again. Matthew grinned at me, "Sorry about that, I forgot we are dealing with utter scum so what can we expect but language like that?"

Periodically Mr F would give a heave and attempt to throw off his captors but neither Liam nor Matthew seemed perturbed by this and kept him in place without much effort, Matthew actually using just one hand at a time while taking selfies with his phone with the other. I made a mental note that instead of trips to the gym I should maybe take up hammering old washing machines to bits.

Geraint and I, wearing gloves from my hair-dyeing kits, looked over the bags, being careful not to make skin contact with them, and sure enough, among the odd streak of green and patch of grey there were thin streaks of reddish-brown up near the tops of two of them.

Time was passing. I checked my phone. I hoped the police were on their way.

"Where is the police station?" someone asked.

"In town – just the other side of the common," was the answer.

In anxiety about the car's arrival, my message

having gone astray and even its maybe missing the house, I went out to the front to see if I could spot them arriving and there I beheld a wonderful sight.

I heard them first of course but it was a sound I could not place although I seem to have known it all my life and then I saw them: around the bend in the road, from off the main road to the common, came three horses cantering. The lowering sun throwing their shadows across the grey asphalt, the shadows of the horses and of the figures they carried, riding bareback, the sound of great feathered hooves echoing off the houses. Megan rode the first piebald, her hands gripping the horse's mane, her own long hair flying behind her. Her expression told me that Mr F was very, very lucky that he would only have the police to deal with. Behind her, riding a skewbald, was Jimmy and sitting behind him, hanging on to Jimmy's waist with both arms for dear life, his helmet lost on the common somewhere, was PC Plum. I did not know this gentleman, we had not discussed our private lives in our several encounters but I knew immediately, from his facial expression and posture, that in a list of his favourite pastimes, horse riding would not come anywhere in the top ten. Behind them, on the third horse, also with a police officer clinging to him with all the closeness and passion of a lover, was Da. The three rode past me and up to the gate, the riders ducking under the frame of the gate and I heard a shout of welcome from the others as they arrived on the scene. I knew then for certain that I would easily have heard, from where I stood, any call that Edith would have made from the garden that evening and knew for certain that she had not called out to her husband as he stood talking to us on the pavement and that she had already, by then, fallen onto the blood-spattered leaves and taken her last breath on this earth..

The police arrested Mr Fitzsimmons, when they had recovered from the momentary confusion that it wasn't the dyed-haired or tattooed people they had to arrest but the be-suited, white gentleman on whom they were sitting, and read him his rights. Matthew lifted him up and stood him upright, the police cut the twine ties and Mr Fitzsimmons made a dash for the gate – falling flat on his face from the tied laces. They were cut too and he sagged visibly as if in defeat but just as the handcuffs were being opened he suddenly erupted into action, ran past the coppers, and headed for the gate, but Megan, stood by the gate with the horses, blocked his exit, knocking him over sideways with the full force of her body. He landed on some cuttings, looking shocked, where he was arrested and handcuffed, then he sort of sagged for real. The police looked at the tell-tale marks that were pointed out to them and wrapped up the bags for forensics to see. Everyone, except Mr Fitzsimmons, had been very careful not to leave any prints on those bags.

"That looks like blood alright," said one, "and if it matches the victims', how else could it have got there?"

The photographer offered them the pictures of Mr F attempting to set the bags alight and of the citizens making the arrest and there were other videos on phones showing everything Mr F had done since arriving in the garden. Mr F was led away in handcuffs with dirt on his face. The police, after a short conversation with me, looked in the BBQ and found small scraps of white cotton at the edge of the burned area which they also took up with tweezers and put into plastic bags. I had no doubt that remnants of blood would be found on them too.

"Isn't it amazing what you can find when you can be bothered to look?" said Liam, quite loudly, eyeing the bags of evidence.

Angela offered to drive police and prisoner to the station in lieu of their car and this was accepted by Plum and his colleagues with some gratitude. Neither officer was walking quite normally, I noticed, as they left.

Later on, back at the site around the fire, with mugs of hot chocolate, we heard how the police car had been rushing across the common and hit a pothole in the shadows – the skills of the driver had prevented an accident but the tyre was burst. The children, gathering wood on the common, had ran to alert their adults 'the police are coming' and, aware of the call the police were responding to, the cavalry had been organised in moments to rescue the police and bring them to their journey's end.

Liam looked at Jimmy.

"You could just as easily have hitched up the buggy and brought the gentlemen in uniform just as quickly and in some comfort, as it is they won't walk straight for a week."

Jimmy took a sip of his cocoa and frowned, "Well now, why didn't I think of that?" he said. "Guess I'm just not clever like you!"

We were still there when Billy and Da got back. Da had, again, gone to fetch a son from the police station. Billy was hugged by everybody and shook hands with us. Angela and I were promised free services and fixings on our car for life and as much fortune-telling as we would ever need. Pearl and Megan hugged us both. As Billy sat with Megan, with their children near them, I felt guilty at my suspicions of him and the others, but did not want to confess them.

"We're going to have to fix up one of them washing machines," said Billy, "to do proper hot washes. Bloodstains off that nazi's nose on my shirt sleeve is what caused all this. Then they found the other. Hand-washing didn't touch it! *Can* washing machines run off batteries?"

"It would have washed off if you hadn't worn it all night on the common! Do your own washing if you have any complaints," said Pearl. "And I'm not having no washing machine. Conk out in a year they do."

They all smiled at her dedication to the old ways.

"That'll teach you to wear protective gear, Billy, like that shop steward's always telling you."

"Yellow's not my colour," said Billy, looking offended.

"Well, next time you break a nazi's nose," said Liam to Billy, "could you just do us all a favour and step aside, not stand there like a big eejit and let him gush all over you? I didn't get any blood on *my* shirt."

"Yeh I noticed that. How *is* your bruise by the way? The idea is, young Liam, that you hit *them*. I'll show you the basics again, shall I?"

I waited for the jousting that then ensued to pause for a chance to ask Billy what I needed to ask.

"Billy," I said, when he and Liam had finished the bout and Liam had rejoined the gathering around the campfire, "how did you know Leon's name? The car-driver? In Buttersville? You knew it before we told you. *How* did you know?"

Billy finished re-fastening his cuffs and smoothing his hair after the tussle with Liam and frowned at me, not comprehending for a moment. "Oh Leon?" he said, remembering who Leon was. He thought for a moment, "Well you were in the flat a while, me and Liam came to the door to see if we could hear anything. We were a bit worried what might be happening in there. There were two doorbells with two name tags – one was 'A. Sinclair' and the other 'Leon Pederson'. We knew he was Pederson from the garage."

He was still frowning, probably wondering why I had asked. I did not feel, at that moment, like enlightening him so I just nodded and said, "Yes, of course. The names on the doorbells," and made a mental note to never, ever try to become a private detective.

Pearl called for a minute's silence and a prayer for the 'poor lady' who had had her life taken from her too soon and we stood quietly in the firelight as Pearl spoke and prayed as dusk fell.

We shook hands and shared some hugs with some and handshakes with others then went back across the common to our house. All was peaceful and quiet in the close.

"It's been quite a week," said Angela. "Now then, it's Monday again, time for another Skype with Hugo and I must ask him about all that stuff Anthea was saying."

I left her to it. It was not my story. It was for me to have guessed it, Anthea to have told it, and for Hugo to confirm. And for Angela to find out something of her own past and something more about people keeping secrets in order to live.

She and Geraint were meeting up again in a few days for a film festival, all-night showing of some favourite franchise or other. She seemed to have found someone who shared her passions and obsessions. I could envisage them spending many happy hours engrossed in the digital and cellulloid world far away from the one through which us lesser mortals had to struggle and wade.

I had already become accustomed to their passionate debates about whether, 'Bend it Like Beckham' or 'Shanghai Noon' was really the best film ever made or whether 'Chocolat', 'Spartacus' or 'Pride' could be usefully compared to 'Black Panther' in its exploration of all that is best in the human spirit. I usually left them to it.

Frank and I had eventually made a date for dinner at one of our favourite restaurants which we hadn't visited for a while. Maybe it was time to go home but maybe also time to make a home. Anthea's story had got me thinking: our own children didn't need us anymore and lived far away but maybe there were others who did; maybe rattling around in that big house on our own was not the best way to be for either of us – too much house and too much loneliness. We were always waiting for our own children and grandchildren to visit but they never did so maybe we had rooms enough for other children who needed someone to care for them. I'd enjoyed being an honorary auntie and we had such a big garden that little ones could play in or teenagers lounge in, though we'd probably have to cover over the pool … I'll talk about it with Frank.

Afterwords

Sowing & Reaping

There were two funerals that week: at one Angela sat with Geraint; Martin sat with Allan, and Frank and I sat alongside them. I don't know if anyone had any problem with any of that as we did not ask. It was a dignified ceremony. We each gave Martin's mother our condolences. Martin and Allan brought Martin's mother in their car and walked with her behind the coffin. Martin had 'come out' to her a few days earlier so maybe now they could begin to get to know each other, and she could welcome her new son-in-law into her life? Hugo had sent flowers from himself and from Mafwaney and the great-grandchildren whom the deceased had never met or even known about. There was a photograph attached to the flowers by way of saying a cautious 'hello'. I saw his mother looking at it in wonder and some dawning of understanding. Angela chatted to her for a while and introduced Geraint and Frank and me and we all said the things that people say at funerals and there was much small talk at the buffet afterwards and anecdotes about the deceased. I saw her shaking hands with Allan and chatting with him and Martin.

Angela and I both also went to Mrs F's funeral. We wanted to say our farewells and felt we owed her that at least. She seemed to have had a miserable, though comfortable, life – married to someone who had abused her then murdered her. It still seemed surreal that something so dreadful had happened/been happening next door to us as we went about our lives but, as Geraint had said, "Two women are murdered every week by their partner or ex-partner so, statistically speaking, it was not at all surreal that one such horror had happened next door to us." The funeral party was mostly family members with a smattering of faces from the Golf Club and was a small gathering. I pondered that maybe if you spend your life hating people who are in any way different from yourself, then there aren't that many left for you to invite into your life. I remembered Elisha Brown's overture of friendship to Edith and the iron bars of prejudice which had kept Edith from responding. I was glad at least we had found her killer and the right man was behind bars. He did not attend her funeral.

Epilogue

A year later, Hugo and Mafwaney and their children were visiting again and it was Spring once more. On the appointed date, along with millions of others around the world, we had our little gathering. There was one going on in town too but Angela very particularly wanted to have one here – all through the house and back-garden and on the front lawn too, and so it was. The puppet show had gone ahead at last in the morning, the neighbourhood's children had indeed attended and met each other, then, in the afternoon, we gathered. Guests arrived, each bringing a dish of food which together made up quite an amazing buffet for us to choose from and share. Martin and Allan had brought a rainbow banner and hung it from the tree's branches; the two who had brought the petition to the meeting came too and this time I remembered their names. Then Billy and Megan, Simon and Fern, Pearl and Da, and some of the children came with cakes which Pearl had made on the fire as the Travellers were again encamped on the common.

Some of the huge stones which had been placed along the side of the road the previous Autumn, to stop anyone parking their trailers or holiday homes on the common, had miraculously crumbled into dust and splinters overnight, almost as if someone had taken a great sledgehammer to them. Leon and his girlfriend were there and Anthea and her boyfriend, Geraint and the photographer, whose name, we discovered, was Georgie. Elisha and Henry Brown were there, chatting to Pearl, sitting in folding chairs brought out and set on the little front lawn in respect for people who didn't like being indoors too much or/and didn't like standing up for too long. Jake and his family were there too. We heard how his employers had tried to sack him for bringing 'bad publicity' to the firm during his run-in with the police when he had been wrongfully arrested for murder, but all his workmates had walked out and refused to return until he had been given it back again. Then there was Frank and me and our two foster-children who joined in playing with all the others. Frank was quite bemused by it all but, enjoying the cakes and ale, wandered about joining in conversations here and there and helped keep an eye on our little Sam and Jasmine, making sure they, too, had their fair share of jelly and cake.

Later, most of us would go up on the common and make an evening of it in the gathering dark there'd be enough of us so the police wouldn't be able to cause any trouble, here and now, Angela said a few words about why we were here, about George Floyd and others, then, those that could do so with a fair chance of being able to get up again, all took the knee. Some of us said a few words about what this meant to us as the sun lowered in the sky, throwing all our shadows across the lawn until they merged and mingled together and we all raised our thoughts to the struggle of each and all of us to be who we are.

BY THE SAME AUTHOR

ALWAYS READ THE SMALL TALK by Beatrice Felicity Cadwallader-Smythe

EXPERT WITNESS: A TESTIMONY: DREAMS by J. Richardson (pen name)

EXPERT WITNESS: A TESTIMONY: AWAKENINGS by J. Richardson (pen name)

MAKING ROOM by J. Richardson (pen name)

Printed in Great Britain
by Amazon

36665816R00185